About

CW00969473

Keith Bullock spent time living in Austria, Iceland Denmark. He majored in Danish and Scandinavian Literature and married a Parisian. Upon leaving a career in educational management he scripted a film for the Cannes Festival of 2008. He now lives part of the year in France. This is his first novel.

For my wife Catherine and my children, Tanya, Marc and David; they are the best one could have, the most loving one could hope for.

Keith Bullock

WINNING TICKET

AUSTIN MACAULEY PUBLISHERS™

LONDON • CAMBRIDGE • NEW YORK • SHARJAH

A CIP catalogue record for this title is available from the British Library.

ISBN 9781786930637 (Paperback)
ISBN 9781786930644 (Hardback)
ISBN 9781786930651 (E-Book)
www.austinmacauley.com

First Published (2017)
Austin Macauley Publishers Ltd.
25 Canada Square
Canary Wharf
London
E14 5LQ

Acknowledgements

Thanks to Kaush Patel for his unflinching support. Thanks also to my brother Paul, and friends: Sohini Kar-Purkayastha, Prakesh Singh, Bill Bailey, Sally Bryan and Barbara and Jim Wilkinson for reading the draft and saying nice things. Thanks to my children's partners: Darren, Ishani and Ariane for their enthusiasm. Special thanks too: to Marie Tsaloumas at the QE Hospital, Birmingham who has done so much for my eyesight and the members of both Malvern U3A Philosophy and Creative Writing Groups for helping with my monthly mental gymnastics. Finally, a big thank you to all at Austin Macauley for their faith in me and unfailing assistance with the manuscript.

1

I'm Dudley through and through, almost third generation. My old man was fourteen when his parents stepped out in a daze from an East African plane. It was nineteen fifty-five and they headed from Heathrow to distant relatives in the Black Country. He attended just one year of secondary school before being taken on by the local foundry. By the time I came along he'd been working as a caster for a full fifteen years. I feel Sikh, but it's difficult to feel Indian. On Dad's side of the family no-one has set foot in Mother India for almost a hundred years. They were in Africa building railways from the earliest days of the British Raj. My mum was from there too, but her family had the sense to leave Uganda long before Idi Amin chucked out the rest in nineteen seventy-two. She died together with my little brother, in childbirth, when I was three. Dad was a very special man, he brought me up alone, with occasional help from Mum's family.

I don't remember Mum, of course, nor Granddad. Granddad was a signed up member of the Khalsa, a fully practising Sikh who kept Kesh, wore Kara, Kanga and Kacha, carried the Kirpan and visited the Gurdwara each day. Dad believed that Granddad didn't come back, that he'd reached Level Five: *Sach Khand* – the final Union with God. It's a nice comforting thought. I can't believe the same of Dad; he was a great father, a good, hard-working bloke but he liked his pint, trimmed his beard and stayed away from our temple, the Gurdwara. It's easy now to understand why: all foundry workers were given a shift beer allowance to counter the sweat they lost, and several of the first Sikhs to enter British foundries met with horrendous industrial accidents when their unshaven beards caught fire from the sparks and furnaces. Blisters on Dad's face and arms and burns to his clothing were almost weekly occurrences.

No more time for daydreams; it's Saturday night; the big push. I go through with the teas. Quite busy already, though nothing compared with what we can expect when the football crowd returns. It's a Prem' League local derby against the Villa – pray God the Baggies won, happy fans splash week-end cash: the Lottery, booze, ciggies and sweets. When push comes to shove, my clientele will always put these above paying the rent.

Jas, is serving 'Me and our Mum', a couple we joke about. He's thirty-five-ish, going on sixty, small, effeminate and joined at the hip to his elderly mother. I could put their weekend order together without them ever having to open their mouths. ('Me and our mum would like eight ounces of liquorice allsorts and two packs of salted peanuts, if you please. And me and our mum would like a bottle of ginger beer and the *Woman's Own.* ')

I pass my wife her tea. The shop's pepping up now – old fellas anxious to get their hands on the racing pages, early troopers from the young lager brigade, single mums mooching for Friday night fast food solutions, nicotine-stained baccy whackers and a ceaseless stream of Camelot big-win dreamers. I cross to the opposite counter where our assistant, Isha, is busy doling out the Lottery tickets and I hand her the second steaming cup.

I'm about to return out back for my own brew when four lads enter. They've drifted over from the flats opposite, the only local tower block left standing. It looks like party time, they're carrying two armfuls apiece of canned lager. Strictly speaking, I should be checking their IDs for age, but if I did much of that around here I'd lose half my takings and get my windows kicked in for good measure.

"Come on, Rakki!" yells Ryan, their spiky-haired leader. "A man could bleeding die of thirst!"

Wayne, Dwayne and Kyle crack up at the World's Greatest Joke. Wayne and Dwayne are chalk and cheese; they're twins, according to their mother. She doesn't look much older than her brood and certainly no wiser. When she was expecting, she'd hoped for triplets for the additional child allowance. The third arrival would have been 'Cain'. 'Gain' would have been more appropriate, I'd say.

Jas is flashing us disapproving glances. Mainly for her benefit, I put on my stern look. "You watch your language now, young Ryan," I tell him.

They're not the brightest stars in the firmament, bless 'em and by a whisker, Kyle twinkles even less brightly than his un-heavenly soul mates. He once asked me good-naturedly whether we were ever going back to Iraq.

"Why Iraq?" I enquired with some surprise.

"Well, your name's Rakki, innit?"

"I know a bloke called Ted Winters," I told him, "So d'you suppose that perhaps he's from the North Pole?"

The four facial expressions before me were reminiscent of the Mayan death masks I've seen at the British Museum.

"So why are you called *Kyle*?" (I'll never know why I persisted.)

"I dunno."

"I think it's Gaelic," I informed him.

"Where's that then?"

"It's not a place, it's Scottish for 'a strip of water'."

"Are you taking the piss? I'm from Dudley."

He's never quite forgiven me.

Back in the present Wayne and Dwayne are cheerfully chorusing: "Come on, Rakki! Come on Rakki! We wanna neck some booze!"

I take their money with a smile and hand over their change. I can see from Jas' face that she expected a more robust reaction. When she's at her lowest, I remind her that we only have to serve them and that some poor sods spend five days a week trying to teach them. I suppose it's difficult to bear that in mind when she's cleaning Saturday-night sick from the front step on Sunday mornings.

There's no denying that our customers are rough and ready, but there's no real harm in them. I grew up with a similar crowd in the nearby streets. It's what I love about the job, the cut and thrust of it all, rolling with the punch, giving 'em back their cheek and backchat. It makes the world go around.

My tea is still out back, it'll be bloody cold by now. No matter. I choose a moment of slack and push through into our pokey living quarters behind the shop. Sangita's gently trying to persuade Amal to work with her on a jigsaw. It's one of *his* jigsaws but he's not in the mood. When he wants to, he can finish them at stunning speed. It's part of his condition: there are areas of his mind that work with the speed of a computer and yet for much of the time he seems incapable of understanding the simplest of instructions. It's not right that his sister should have to take so much responsibility for him, but it's the only way that Jas and I get a break from it when he's at home. God knows what we'll do next year if she gets into the Royal College of Music.

Time to cut the mental dilly-dally, the shop must be filling up. I cross and give my darling Sangi a quick cuddle. She's a little miracle worker, my daughter. It breaks me up to think of her with her violin, making such beautiful music in our tiny box-room. What inspiration can there be in a view of the corrugated roofs of two engineering factories? If I had my way, she'd have a light and airy music room looking out over a rose garden.

The place is humming! I get a look from Jas that says I've been out back too long. My God, how she *hates* the shop! A bus from West Brom' has dropped off the first wave of jubilant fans. Many have had a skinful at the match and the atmosphere in the shop is soon tinged with the odour of stale lager. Six or seven of the first in have scooped up their evening booze supplies and are approaching the counters. I hasten to intervene – too late, they're heading for Jas.

"Come – on – the – Bagg--ies!!" screams the group simultaneously.

Jas is only half their size but she eyeballs them fiercely.

"Can you please show a little respect for other customers and keep the noise down!" she shouts. Ironically, she's almost matched their decibels. There's menace in her demeanour and the piercing stare from those dark brown eyes could stop trains on Indian level crossings and send sacred cows running for the hills. The macho rabble quietens but one brave soldier has the temerity to put his fingers to his lips and make mock-shushing noises. He's a good two feet taller than Jas, but she's around the counter in an instant and fixes him with a death stare. He's not looking so cocky now and Jas makes sure that they all have to wait on her convenience for their booze and fags.

I'm embarrassed, but there's no doubting her spunk. These are guys who might well have blood on their boots from the skulls of rival Villa supporters. They leave, chastened and sobered and Jas throws me another deeply reproachful look. It probably conveys that I was expected to draw upon my ancestry, leap from behind the counter, unsheathe my kirpan and slash them into a thousand pieces.

It pains me, but in the five years that we've owned the shop, she's never known a day's happiness. The problem's not easily solved. When I chucked my job as a postman we sank every last penny into this venture and mortgaged ourselves up to the eyeballs. There's no way back into the Post, jobs there are as rare as chapattis in Chattanooga. I just thank God that she's no real idea of just how much debt we're in. Sooner or later, we'll have to get out. I can't stand by for ever, watching her diminish by the day. But why is life so perverse? Despite all of the debt, and all of the worries, from the minute we moved in, I came alive. I'm a born trader, a wheeler-dealer. I identify with the business: it's *me*.

Back to the fray. I'm in the middle of serving Pop Richardson with his daily ounce of Old Holborn when I hear Jasvinder's voice rise again. She's eye to eye with Two Ton Tess – a fat, greasy-haired woman whose name I've never bothered to retain.

"I've told you more than once, Mrs Yarnall, we don't do credit."

"So, that's OK then? My kids can bleedin' starve tonight, can they?" cries the indignant woman.

No, no – don't rise to it, Jas, I'm thinking – but of course, she does.

"Well perhaps you should have thought of that when you bought your cigarettes earlier in the week," says Jas.

"Cheeky cow! I'll spend my money on what I likes," shouts TTT. Her face seems to have swollen to twice its normal pancake size and she's turning towards the queue behind her, in the hope of mustering client solidarity.

"Yes, but not *my* money, Mrs Yarnall," says my redoubtable wife.

Notwithstanding the moral superiority of my wife's argument and its reflection of a mutually agreed commercial strategy, I fear that the confrontation is rapidly attaining critical mass and I cross the shop at warp speed.

"Look, what is it that you actually need to purchase?" I enquire.

"Just a mini-pack of your over-priced fish fingers, a loaf and a bleeding tin of beans," comes the reply.

I keep my gaze firmly away from Jasvinder and dismiss the frightful image of haemorrhaging bean cans.

"Well on the basis that you may have misunderstood our policy, we're going to make a one-off exception for you tonight, you may have a ten pound credit until Tuesday."

"In that case you can add ten Silk Cut," says the resourceful behemoth.

I know my wife is furious, she stalks off to serve somebody else and leaves me to enter the woman's items into the till. By an act of Providence, Jas is fully occupied and fails to notice when finally the fat lady sweeps triumphantly from the premises.

When it rains, it pours... Jas is moving on towards Tom Andrews. He's one of our regulars, a down and out who lives in a Salvation Army hostel at the end of the road. Tom's usually a mild-mannered type, so it's out of character for him to be tapping a two litre cider bottle heavily and rhythmically against the counter top. Frequently, we see him the worse for wear, but up to now he's never been any trouble. I've got him pegged as an educated guy who's fallen on hard times but he hasn't told me that directly and I've never asked.

As Jas approaches, he's still banging down his cider bottle and looking extremely unhappy. It must be a reaction to the delay caused by our mini-drama with the dowdy diva. If he's throwing down a challenge to my missus, he's on a very slippery wicket – I can see that customer relations have tumbled progressively to the basement of her commercial agenda.

"You prefer cider when it's exploded all over you then, Mr Andrews?" she enquires.

"I'd have preferred it a couple of hours ago, when I first got to the till," he replies.

Oh dear, oh dear, oh dear.

"No doubt you saw how busy we've been," says Jas. "Or are you late for a board meeting?"

"That's nice. That's very nice," says Tom, holding his own.

I go over at a gallop, urgently fixing my most winsome smile. Jas sees me coming.

"Oh, to hell with it!" she shouts and turns on her heel. Bang! Goes the door to our private quarters. One or two packets of fags fall from the shelves. She's gone.

"Sorry about that," I mutter. "Will it be just the cider?"

"It's *Saturday*," says Tom and affects a dramatic pause. He's apparently under the impression that I'm clairvoyant. I can see that he's had more than a few drinks already. "You *know*. My lottery ticket."

Isha has overheard and prints me one. I take Tom's money and he shambles over to collect his ticket. She's a great girl, Isha, only nineteen, quiet, efficient and hardworking. Outside the shop, sport is her life: netball, hockey and women's cricket – fairly unusual for an Asian girl.

"Is Jas OK?" she asks me, when finally we have a break in the stream.

"If it's all right with you, I'll just nip through and see."

I put my head around the door to our tiny dining and living area, intent on a peace pow-wow. Sangita's on the settee reading a borrowed copy of *Hello!* from the shop.

Jas throws me yet another dirty look; she's at the table helping Amal. We're not advised to spoon-feed him but he'll sit there all day sometimes, staring at his plate. It's tiresome, frustrating, gut-wrenching.

"We're just about to start cashing up," I announce. "Should be through in about twenty minutes."

"Well you can get your own food, I've *had* it. I'm going to bed when I've finished with him."

Amal is rocking backwards and forwards on his chair. It's something he *does*. There's a dent beginning to appear on the freshly emulsioned wall behind him. Against my better judgement, I let it get to me.

"Can't you stop him doing that? There'll be no bloody wall left."

No one is allowed to knock Amal. Jas doesn't move a muscle but flashes me another salvo, from tonight's burgeoning armoury of hostile looks. Sangita springs to her feet with tears in her eyes and puts a protective arm around her brother's shoulders. I feel wretched, but I'm on a short fuse now and I step backward and slam the door shut from the shop side.

Isha has put up the 'Closed' sign and as she walks back to the counter she gives me her special enquiring look. I needed no prompting, I know I have to return and smooth things over. I sigh, throw my arms theatrically into the air and push back through the interior door. I'm now looking at the two finalists in *The World's Unhappiest Face Contest* and there's not an eyelash to choose between them.

"Look, I'm sorry."

I go over and put an arm around Amal.

"Once we've closed up tomorrow, how about we go over to Himley Hall after lunch? The forecast's good and we could all use the fresh air?"

Sangita pulls a bit of a face, but Jas nods, almost imperceptibly. The way to her heart is through Amal. We all know he's fascinated by flowers, he can spend forever tramping around staring at individual blooms, it's been one of his few abiding interests.

"There's some dhal in the fridge, you can warm it up," she says, by way of a truce.

By the time Isha and I have balanced and closed the safe, it's ten o'clock. I see her to the door and wave to her dad sitting out there in his car. They're a nice Hindu family, a little stricter on Isha than we are with Sangita, but that's their way – it takes all sorts.

"See you Monday!" I shout.

Isha doesn't work Sundays. On Sundays, Jas and I manage alone and close up at one o'clock. Half a day off a week and then, frequently, there's stock to order, or the occasional problem with a balance carried over. I worked it out once – I do an average of ninety-seven hours a week – that's well over double the hours I did as a postman and lately, I'm not even covering our costs.

I lock up and go through to the lounge. They're all in bed. I know exactly what I'm going to do next. In the light of the austerity regime I'm imposing, it's unfair, but I've rationalised: it's once in a blue moon and I *deserve* it, it's medicinal, it keeps me sane and it's well under control. I return to the shop and take a bottle of Bell's whisky from the shelf.

The microwaved dhal tastes good. I eat it with my fingers, dipping pieces of wholemeal bread into its savoury interior; not traditional, but the way I like it. Between mouthfuls I pour whisky, three fingers at a time, topped with a finger of water. My mind quietens and my body relaxes. Jas will find the half-empty bottle in the morning. She may feel resentful, but it's doubtful that she'll say anything. At the end of the day, *I'm* the head of the bloody household. If I feel like a drink, I'll *have* a bloody drink.

I get to thinking about what kind of a Sikh I am. Pretty good, in general I believe, but then again, that's one of the forbidden sins: Pride – and there's been another one to feel guilty about today: Anger. But seriously, I believe in the one God of all things and that all men are created equal and I try hard to uphold the moral values I've learned. I'm a good family bloke and I've never lusted after other women.

I can feel the whisky beginning to work. Why am I so screwed up? I know I'm not supposed to be attached to material things and that I should |practise contentment, but is it really asking too much to want to get out of the economic hole that we're in?

I pour another shot and down it quickly.

The great thing about Sikhism is, it is gentle, forgiving and all-embracing – There's even a term for people like me: *Sahajdhari* – slow adapters. I haven't yet committed to the Khalsa and don't follow the five K's, even though I do wear the turban most of the time.

Jas never dwells much on matters spiritual; maybe it's because she's so grounded in the here and now and doesn't feel the need? She's the genuine article, an *Indian* Sikh from the Punjab. I went over there for her and brought her back to all this. It wasn't exactly an arranged marriage, but in a way it was: Dad was terminally ill from the foundry fumes and trying to claw back elements of his culture. To please him, I agreed to review three eligible young ladies selected for me back in the Punjab by more spiritually-minded friends of his at the Gurdwara. I met Jasvinder over there by chance. She was best friend to Potential Wife Two and the prettiest of them all: clever too, the only girl in her village ever to win an open scholarship and full board to a public school in Amritsar. If anything, her English is better than mine. I didn't win any medals with the marriage brokers of Dudley of course, in fact, most of them still don't speak to me, but I did find the love of my life. As for the old man, he died happy because no one had the heart to tell him that I'd upset local planning and plucked a different apple from the tree.

The warm glow has spread all over. I could sit here all night and see off the bottle. Jas, Jas, Jas – what the fuck am I going to do? Maybe in India, you would have achieved your full potential? I don't like to think too much about that – you married *me*. You're feisty, honest and hard-working, the mother of my two kids and still as beautiful as the day of our wedding in Amritsar. I know now that putting you behind a counter in Netherton was like planting a rare orchid in a nettle patch. If only you could see that Dudley folk aren't the enemy. Your enemy's your inability to go with the flow – and to dream you married a foreign prince, rather than a poor bastard from Netherton who's doing his best to keep our heads above water.

I reach again for the bottle. Bloody hell! What happened to it all? I must have missed the glass a couple of times – I take a panicky look at the carpet and the sofa cushions, but there's no evidence of spillage.

So, how can I make things right for her? How can I return us to the happiness we knew in the early days? To put it another way: how do we quit our small Indian news agency and grocery shop in the rougher part of Dudley and start over again? The accommodation is tied to the job, our mortgage is crippling and we've bank loans and outstanding debts to suppliers. I feel like a rat in a trap. God knows I've tried. I've pulled the plug on all but the most vital elements of our expenditure and it's still touch and go whether we can even hang on to Isha. Without her, I think we'd sink anyway.

When I worked on the Post, Jas took pleasure in sending money back home. It was never more than a few quid here and there, but in the Punjab that's the difference between whether your kid can go to the village school or not, or whether Jas's old Uncle Gurdip can get the odd bottle of jollop for his stomach ulcer. That's had to go – temporarily, of course. We've argued. Jas refuses to look at the bank statements or to attempt to understand the financial issues. That's probably what started her depression. She's had to cancel her gym membership too and she moans that she's lost her circle of friends. Some *friends,* I say, if it's all down to money. Very un-Sikh-like. But then, that's not entirely honest of me either. How many times have I seen mates down at the Gurdwara lately? Most of the buggers I grew up with seem to be doing pretty well and it kind of rubs against the grain a little.

It's the alcohol talking now, I realise I'm just a conduit. It's never made me fierce and nasty – I drink to think. Sadly, it's an aspiration that's subject to the Law of

Diminishing Returns. I'm long past *sharp and reflective* and I'm drifting rapidly out of *maudlin* into *foggy and confused*. Alcohol of course, is one of the four *kurahits:* an absolute bloody no-no, even though most of us indulge. I'm feeling bad about that too – am I just some massive hypocrite? I hope not, I'm Sikh to the core, but just like Dad used to say about himself: I'm not yet ready for the Khalsa, the demands of everyday life get in the way too much.

The demands of life … *Shit!* It's half past midnight and Sunday's a five o'clock start, counting out the paper rounds before the delivery kids arrive. I creep upstairs and undress clumsily. Jas is snoring gently. I slip in beside her. I brush against her bum which is stationed well over on my side of the bed and I feel a twinge of desire. It's enough to sober me, I'm now on a baser mission and clear as a bell – no pun intended with Bell's – and eagerly I wriggle closer to her musky warmth.

"You've been drinking," she murmurs and straightens herself. It has the effect of creating a six inch divide between us and immediately, I feel myself shrinking.

I have to tell myself, she said *drinking* – fool – nothing to do with *shrinking!* She must have the nose of a search and rescue hound, my wife – and now, her bum might as well be an iceberg and me the marauding Titanic. Well – just as long as we don't become ships that pass in the night. I'm stupidly pleased with my drunken extended metaphor, it makes up for the shrinking/drinking confusion. Just as well, as it's the only satisfaction I'm going to get tonight. Come to think of it, our lovemaking's been like the Dover ferry lately: roll on, roll off. Hah! *Sheer genius!* King of Wit. I'm grinning like an idiot in the darkness.

My head's beginning to spin, so I turn over away from her. I've always loved words, words and word play – at school it was the only thing that I was any good at. I remember Mr Montgomery telling the English Language class: 'Basra is bound for greatness – our first brown Shakespeare.' It was my proudest moment.

Oh fuck, who am I kidding? It's as much as I can do nowadays to write out the tobacco order. I'm a snuffed-out candle, a busted flush and I feel as miserable as sin. Sikh to the core. I'm bloody *sick* to the core. I close my eyes at that, it's just one pun too many … one pun too many … one pun too many…

The alarm clangs in my left ear and I leap for it like a cat on a sparrow. *I can't believe it!* I've only just shut my bloody eyes! My head's banging and my mouth feels like the bottom of a birdcage. I'm full of toxins and feeling ill. The four Sunday paper rounds are waiting to be counted, it's the only morning we deliver. Jas sleeps on. I'm feeling sorry for myself and it's a sentiment I hate. I stumble through to the bathroom and shower quickly. After I've towelled off, I reach for the barrier cream and cover my arms. Don't know why I bother, it doesn't seem to prevent the eczema; by the end of an hour's newspaper-counting my hands and arms are black with newsprint, rough as sandpaper and as cracked as the earth of Bihar. 'You must wear gloves, Mr Basra,' my GP tells me. He's never tried counting Sunday newspapers. Wearing gloves, I'd be counting 'em until Monday.

I'm just about through marking up the rounds and on my second cup of tea when the paper kids knock the front door. They're a lively, cheeky bunch – Sean and Marie, a carrot-haired brother and sister aged fourteen and fifteen, and Lee and Sting, both sixteen, street-wise and shaven-headed. 'Sting' – I get to wondering about Netherton parents and names again: where on earth did *that* label originate? Why not 'Itch' or 'Irritate'? I'm guessing it *is* his real birth name, for no one ever calls him anything else. What matters however is that they're a good team and reliable. I used to have eight rounds, but when they began demolishing the tower blocks around here it cost me dear. It looks like the Syrian front-line out there these days.

Jas comes through at seven thirty and I go and grab the quick breakfast that she's left out for me. No mention of last night's booze. So far, so good. Once I get into my rhythm, I quite like Sunday mornings. The luckiest of the boozers are still in bed, the rest are draped over street bollards, in A&E, or waiting to be released from overnight cells. More to the point, they're not in *here* and the abstinent minority are so much easier to handle. Jas is relaxed, there's sometimes time for a chat with people and ahead, there's the prospect of a few hours to ourselves.

Sangita and Amal are up early and having breakfast with me. Sangi tells Amal that we're going to Himley this afternoon. I think I see a reaction in his eyes, but I'm *always* seeing reactions in his eyes. I rise from the table, give my daughter a squeeze and ask her if she's slept all right.

"I'm worried, Dad," she tells me. "What if I never get into the RCM?"

The RCM, I've learned, is the Royal College of Music. She has to present the first part of a concerto and some other backing music at an audition next year, if she's to have any chance of gaining admission.

"You will, darling, I'm sure. You just have to keep up with the practising."

"But Dad, you don't understand!" Dads never do, I've learned. "I don't do *enough.* I need to start going to practice sessions on Saturdays in Birmingham."

"We'll sort it," I tell her. "But, Love, I have to get back to the shop right now."

I see her beautiful face fall and my heart falls with it. She wants me to be more supportive – a hands-on dad – but I'm always pushed for time and full of worries. Or perhaps it's just that I don't want to think that far ahead?

"We'll sort it, I promise," I repeat and kiss her on the forehead, wondering how the hell we can ever *sort it.* Without Sangita to watch Amal on Saturdays, we'd be totally up the creek. Just once a month we get some relief, when he's 'on the house' as they call it, for a weekend. I'm guessing that one Saturday's practice in four in Birmingham, won't be enough to guarantee that Sangi makes the grade.

I go through. The shop's quite busy. An early morning surge – a group of anglers on their way to a fishing contest in Bewdley (pipe tobacco, chocolate and lemonade), a couple of shift workers coming back off nights (fags and the *Sunday Mirror),* a few other early birds in for newspapers, fags, loaves of bread, packets of cereals, margarine and jam. Jas and I work our way through them. I'm still trying to gauge her temperature: she seems fine with the customers this morning. Mrs Kumar enters. I'm not too keen on her – too much of a gossip – but she and Jas get on well. For the next ten minutes, whilst they chat, I'll be doing the donkey work. At least, there are no rowdy youths in to light her fuse.

I'm serving Fred Johnson, he's a Jamaican bus driver. It's *complicated*: he wants to pay his papers but it's been five weeks and the book's not up to date. Two of his kids have comics, his wife takes three knitting magazines but reckons that she's not had two of them for a fortnight, he takes a racing paper in addition to the *Daily Mirror* which he wants to change for *The Sun* and his missus paid four quid against the bill last Friday. They're the kind of issues that take forever to sort out and *always* end with me losing money.

Out of the corner of my eye, I see our boozy friend Tom Andrews walk in. Unusual for a Sunday morning, he must have found some additional cider money from somewhere. He looks grim: unshaven, sallow and unkempt. Uncharacteristically, Jas breaks off from her natter with Mrs Kumar and heads towards him. I can see from her face that she's not forgotten the previous evening. I daren't intervene for a second time. *Please, please, God, keep the lid on things.*

"How can I help you?" she asks.

I'm pleased – that sounded civil enough.

Tom nods in my direction. "I'll wait," he tells her.

Jas shrugs nonchalantly. "Suit yourself." She turns and heads back to Mrs Kumar.

Sweet relief! I feel as though an Exocet missile with my name on it just passed by, with GSP failure. I've totally forgotten Fred Johnson and the financial complexities of his newspaper account and I exhale so forcibly that three of his receipt counterfoils blow straight off the counter.

"Whoops! You OK dere, Mista Basra?" he asks in his wonderful sing-song accent.

Tom wanders over to the booze shelves. He returns with a four-pack of Bulmer's. I hasten to finish off quickly with Fred; it's well worth the four quid loss.

"Right," I say at last. "Will it be just the cider?"

Tom fishes in his shirt pocket with his dirty finger nails. "And can you check last night's ticket?"

I take his money and his ticket. He could have bloody-well checked it for himself – the winning numbers are there on the wall, staring him in the face. I have a Camelot display board and four times a week I post the lottery winning numbers: Wednesday and Saturday – the Euro', Thursday and Sunday – the National. I pass him his change and double-check what I'm seeing on the board and on his ticket: *the numbers are identical!*

"I couldn't face the dragon this morning – too much of a hangover."

I don't really catch what he's saying, my heart is pounding so loudly in my ears. Jas is on the way over for some reason: I'm dimly aware that she's looking pissed off. I tear my gaze from the ticket again and see she's eye-balling him.

"What did you say?" Jas demands.

"If you *don't* mind – I was talking to your husband."

"Rakesh! Are you just going to stand there and allow this man to insult me?"

"Yes," I say. Oh, God Almighty … the numbers are *identical!*

"*Yes?*" she demands.

I look up briefly from the ticket. She seems absolutely furious. I wonder vaguely what in hell's upset her now.

"Did you say, 'Yes'?"

"No, I mean, *no.* Look, listen, both of you, there's something -"

"I was having a private conversation, here," Tom is saying.

"Read that notice!" shouts Jas, pointing towards the till. "It tells the *world* that no member of staff here will tolerate abuse!"

I try to gather my wits, to ground myself. "But Jas... I'm sure he was only -"

It's too little, too late. Jas is incandescent. "Get out of my shop!" she orders.

Tom picks up his cans and tries to retain some final vestige of dignity by brushing real or imagined fluff from the sleeve of his threadbare coat.

"I don't *have* to shop here, you know."

"No, you certainly don't!" says my spitfire wife.

He heads for the door and Jas follows, arms akimbo. I follow Jas, still clutching the ticket. There seems to be no real opportunity to intervene.

At the doorway, he seals his fate: "You really are a dragon," he mutters.

I have to take hold of Jas' arm to restrain her, she's already half way over the step and would have followed him outside.

"We can do without you drunken riff-raff!" she shouts at his back. "Get off with you and don't come back!"

"Jas, *Jas,*" I shout, "that's *enough!*"

She's totally lost it. "And you can just get off me, Rakesh! That was a question of honour! You *dare* to let that man insult me!"

She breaks free and flies through to our private quarters. Mrs Kumar, who has stood and witnessed it all, now walks haughtily past me with a look of total contempt. I'm left standing alone, the shop empty of customers.

"Oh, my God! What do I do?" I exclaim out loud. I sprint back to the shop door. Tom is about fifty yards away, heading towards his hostel, swigging from one his cans. For a second I think of pursuing him down the street, but I can't leave the shop and the tills.

"Oh my God!" I repeat to myself, trying to catch my breath. I return to the displayed numbers and check and double check. I put the ticket down, close my eyes and try again to control my breathing. I grab the ticket once more, hold it in trembling fingers and re-check. There is not a shadow of doubt, *it's the winning ticket from the Saturday Lottery.*

There's no sign of Jas. I know I'm in no state to face another customer. It's only just after ten, but I hurry over, pull the blinds and turn around the 'Open' sign to 'Closed'. In the half-light remaining, I take out the small steps from behind the sweet counter and place them next to the high shelf where we keep the adult magazines. The formica up there is loose on the shelf and in need of replacement. Carefully, I place Tom's winning ticket between the shelf and the formica and descend the steps.

I realise that I've been repeating 'Oh, my God,' over and over again and I force myself to stop. I've no idea why I've hidden the ticket, no idea of what to do next. Should I tell Jas? Go around to the hostel? Could I keep it? – I dismiss the thought immediately, it would be a criminal act. But who's to know?

Jas is surprised to see me but too angry to admit it.

"I'm feeling ill Jas," I tell her. "I've had to close up early."

She turns over the page of her newspaper so savagely that it falls to the floor, causing her to mouth a swearword as she bends to collect it. She's still refusing to look in my direction. "Well, *I'm* not bloody-well going back in there, if that's what you think?"

Inwardly, I bristle. When I first met her in India, she would never have dreamt of acting like that, least of all with her husband. Over there, a wife could get herself killed for less. I force myself to calmness. We're *not* 'over there' – nor would I ever want to live by those values. Her words are only slightly less hard to swallow. I remind myself that she's struggling with the lifestyle, struggling under the shadow of our debts.

"Look Jas, can we just cool down? Let's do what I suggested, go to Himley Hall this afternoon and try to put things back together again. We can discuss it all there, out in the fresh air."

She softens slightly, enough to put down the newspaper and look at me. There is still anger but it's tinged with concern. "And you've really had to close the shop?"

It's an opportunity to divert my anger. "*Bugger* the shop for half a day! I know we'll lose on the newspapers and we'll have some explaining to do, but nobody's going to *die* from lack of a newspaper, or a packet of fags. I just can't face any more this morning and I know you've had enough too."

"But we can't afford to do *that* very often."

"Let's just call it a one off. Try to get ourselves mended."

"So, where are you poorly?"

"Everywhere and bloody nowhere, nothing that a few hours in Himley Park won't cure."

We lapse into silence. Neither of us has tried quite hard enough to fully restore normal relations. She goes off to make lunch and I interrupt Sangita's violin practice to tell her we're going out earlier than planned. We gather around the table. To speed things along, Jas has settled for open chicken sandwiches and ice cream from the shop fridge. I spice the top of my sandwich with too many dried chilli flakes from a defective sprinkler, my head explodes and my eyes begin to run. I'm coughing and sneezing and Amal is looking at me quizzically with his big, brown eyes. It breaks some of the remaining tension. Sangi thinks it's hilarious and even Jas manages a reluctant smile. I'll probably survive if I can drink a hundred or so gallons of water.

As Jas showers and prepares for the outing, I sit on the end of the bed, my mind doing overtime again. The way to God is through our actions – and what have I done? Pinched a poor man's lottery ticket. *Not true!* I'm simply safekeeping it until I can get it to him. I should cancel the Himley Hall trip right now and take a walk down to his hostel. I should remain true to my faith: the way to God is through *contentment,* satisfaction with one's lot – fighting the enemy of Envy, and not lusting after the good fortune of other men. But to hell with it, all that can wait until Monday. Tom will be too hooked on his cider to take much notice before then and when he gets the thirst again, he's sure to be back breaking Jas' exclusion order. I can give him the accursed ticket next time I see him.

What's a guy like that going to do with so much money, anyway? Out! Out! Ignoble thought!

I creep downstairs to the lounge and check with the telly. My instinct was right: there's just one single big winner on yesterday's draw. I *have* to check again. Back in the shop I rc-climb the steps and stare at the numbers on the ticket: 8, 17, 22, 31, 37, 39: there can be no doubt about it, *it's the Jackpot.* My legs go to rubber and I'm in danger of falling down the steps.

In spite of Dudley's dark, satanic sweat-shop reputation, we're spoiled for choice when it comes to beautiful surroundings. There's canal walks with herons and swans, the Clent Hills just twenty minutes away with panoramic views across the West Midlands, Bewdley and the River Severn, Kidderminster and its safari park, the Wyre Forest, the Malvern Hills, Cannock Chase – all within easy reach. We chose Himley Hall for Amal, he's easier to control there and fascinated by the gardens, it's also the closest. We pull into the car park and Sangita tells us she's learned that Charles the First once stopped by on his way to the Battle of Bosworth. Apparently, it was landscaped by some guy called Capability Brown; *Capability* Brown – I wish I was Capability Someone, instead of bloody *Incapability* Basra.

Sangi wants to go straight to the log cabin for tea and cake. I have to remind her that we've only just arrived, she's never been a great one for walking. First we'll look at the gardens to spark up Amal, then there'll be a walk around the great lake. I'm hoping it will lift Jas' spirits. Then there'll be time enough for tea and cake.

We walk past the entrance to the nine-hole miniature golf course.

"Remember we used to borrow some clubs and have a go at that? You were good," I remind Jas. She nods. She isn't going to reward me with any enthusiasm, even though she loved the game.

"You and Mum, played?" Sangi enquires incredulously. She has the normal teenage difficulty in imagining that Mum and Dad could have done *anything,* pre-Sangita.

"They lend you a driver, two irons and a putter," I tell her. "Mum used to beat the pants off me."

Sangi snorts her disbelief and I get no corroboration from Jas, who has lapsed back into silence. We walk on and Sangi asks me to explain the strange names I've given to golf clubs. I'm not sure whether it's genuine interest or a test. She breaks off every now and again to chase after her brother like a working collie. It's remarkable how Amal comes alive at the sight of plants and flowers. I'm always thinking he's on the edge of a breakthrough into genuine communication, but it never quite happens. We tour the lake and he's in his shell again, no significant interest, not even in the cute little baby ducklings paddling like crazy to stay in their mother's wake.

Finally, we sit at an outside table and I order refreshments. Jas is still under a cloud, not exactly a storm cloud, more like a dull mist. Amal scoffs two cakes. At one point he has so much in his mouth that he's in danger of choking. Jas hardly seems to notice. When he takes off to stare at a nearby flower bed, Sangita shadows him and my wife chooses her moment.

"You never really support me, do you Rakki?"

I'm shocked. I hadn't seen that one coming and it's not at all the image I have of myself.

"Jas, I do, I'm *always* there for you! How can you even think that?"

"What do they have to do then: knock me down, kick me, rape me before you notice?"

"Jas! What are you *talking* about? Who? When?"

"The football yobs, Mrs Yarnall, the alkie I chucked out – all in the space of one weekend and right under your nose. You should stand up for me, wade in and defend my honour."

"Tom? – He's not an alkie, just a homeless bloke who drinks," I say, sheepishly. It's not the response she was looking for, but Tom Andrews is at the forefront of my mind.

"Oh for God's sake! I'm talking about *you – us,* not him! Rakesh, whatever's gotten into you?"

"Calm down! There's been a lot on my mind lately."

I knew it wasn't over, even though we'd cleared the air before lunch the storm clouds were never far away.

"Does that explain the whisky then?"

That one, I *had* been expecting.

"It's an occasional need. It calms me down, keeps me sane."

"I'm not challenging your right to drink – whatever our faith says about that – but what about your austerity regime? It doesn't stretch as far as whisky, obviously! Me, I can't send money home, I can't go to the gym, I can't afford *anything,* according to you!"

I'm on the edge now too. "Give me a break, Jas, that's unfair! You know *why* we're having to be careful; it won't last forever. The whisky's *occasional,* once in a blue moon!"

"Well, I'll have to find something *occasional* too," she says, childishly.

We lapse into a new silence. Sangita and Amal are holding hands walking around the flower beds. Sangi has spotted that there's an issue between her mum and dad and she's giving us some breathing space. She's amazing.

Jas changes tack. "I don't know how much more of the shop I can take, Rakesh."

It's less of a statement, more of an invitation for me to engage in a mutual Basra life-style audit.

"I know it's tough right now," I say. "I've been thinking: if you really feel you can't take the shop, how about doing some office temping? If you covered the price of another assistant we could stay cash neutral?"

She shrugs non-commitally.

"Come on, Jas, I'm trying to think constructively here. How about it?"

"It might work, I suppose. Things have moved on – I don't know whether I'm up to working in the modern office."

"Of course you are!"

"It's not just about me you know? How can you be happy bringing up the kids in that dump of a shop?"

On another day, I'd have been more than half-inclined to agree with her; today, it hits me as a put-down to all I've strived for.

"Come on Jas, it's hardly a dump! Things aren't *that* bad. The sun's shining, we have our health, our family, each other." They're platitudes, but none the less for that.

She sighs. "I dreamed of so much more, you know. The village girl from Amritsar who met the visiting English millionaire."

"Some millionaire! It'll get better though. Times are hard, people are spending less. I've always said – when they start building the new flats opposite, our takings will –"

"Oh Rakesh, please! I've heard it so often, I'm just sick of it!"

Now, I'm feeling really angry and resentful. Angry with the bloody local council for turning our area into a wasteland and knocking shit out of our takings, resentful of Jas for not making the time and effort to familiarise herself with the economics of our situation. Angry with her for being so basically pessimistic and insensitive. Somehow, I manage to keep the lid on.

"Whatever you say, we have to beat the negative equity – that's pure economics. We wait for an upturn, then we can start thinking of real alternatives. Maybe I should take a leaf out of our customers' book: start doing the National Lottery?"

She sighs heavily again. "Mum said from the beginning you were a dreamer. I should have listened. What about her cataracts, we were set to pay for the treatment? *Look at us:* can't go on holiday, can't replace the car, can't treat ourselves to the gym, or the pub, can't even pay the bills, you tell me. What are we going to do? How in hell will we get Sangita through music college? What about Amal, what kind of chance in life are we going to give *him*?"

Amal's problem is ASD – it's short for Autistic Spectrum Disorder. I'd never heard of it before his diagnosis, we just noticed that from his earliest days, you could seldom get through to him. He looked through you, made noises and got on with his own thing. Bringing him up's been like a slow-motion car crash: first you had a tiny worry about early infant responses, then it began to hit you that he didn't seem to have normal baby reactions, then came tantrums, fits and constant screaming. He came out of much of that at around five, but by then, there were new challenges, no real language development, fixations, rocking, head banging and social withdrawal. It's all to do with his perception of reality – he can't 'read' other people the way we do and therefore he can't work out the appropriate responses. The result is massive permanent frustration with the world.

His diagnosis brought us some relief. At least we were able to put a name to the poor lad's problems. Autism West Midlands has a branch in Dudley and the staff has been great. He was statemented and he goes to a school for autistic children. It was a shock to discover just how many like him there are out there. For our part, we had to learn how to handle his challenging behaviour without anger, frustration or depression. That's the theory! *Of course* we get angry, frustrated and depressed – and desperate and fearful – for his future. He's our little Amal and I'd give *everything* to hear him say, 'Hello, Dad,' like other kids can.

It's below the belt, she knows I have no answer. What indeed will become of him if we never have the money to provide? It pains me like a stake through the heart. 'Singh' means *Lion* – I'm her lion, Sangi's lion, Amal's lion. I should be their protector, the bringer of all comforts and rewards.

"He's in the right special school," I reply. It's a weak-as-shit answer, but it's all I have – other than to tell her to go out and get a bloody full-time job!

She's not finished yet. "And don't you think that the rich would have done so much more? Tutors, specialist equipment, an environment where he could have begun to grow and develop, instead of being stuck in a couple of shoe-box rooms behind a bloody sweet shop?"

She begins to weep.

I'm furious; trapped, cornered, frustrated. "Can you stop carping on about the shop? – It's hardly a bloody *sweet shop*, Jas. Like I said, I'll have to start doing the Lottery."

She jumps to her feet enraged. "If you mention the bloody Lottery again, I swear I'll walk out of this park and you'll never see me again!"

Sangita runs over and places a protective arm around her mother's shoulders. Jas is crying openly and buries her head in our daughter's neck. I give Sangi an open palms sign of defeat and despair. Struggling to control my anger, I stride over to rescue my innocent little boy from the flower beds. I walk him around whilst Sangita does her best to calm her mother. So much for the ambrosial effects of Himley Park! I drive us home in silence, my mind buzzing like a hornet between my ears. I'm sitting on a winning ticket worth several million quid, the answer to all of our prayers. What in *Merry Fuck's* name do I do? It could change everything.

Some Sikh, I tell myself. I don't defend the weak, I covet my neighbour's wealth, I drink, I've stopped giving to charity, I ignore the needs of Jas's family, I don't visit the temple, I don't follow the five K's and I couldn't be feeling more pessimistic – yes, *pessimistic!!!* And I don't have to remind myself that *optimism* is yet another key demand of our faith.

2

It's early Tuesday evening. Sangi's home from school and practising upstairs. The school mini-bus has just dropped off Amal and Jas will need to go through and look after him, whilst Isha and I see off the last hour of the shopping day. There's been no sign of Tom since Sunday. I've imagined him dead in a thousand different ways: he's choked on his cider bottle, he's cut his throat whilst shaving, he's tripped and stumbled under the wheels of the Number 18 bus, he's been set upon by a homicidal hostel dweller, he's fallen down a flight of stairs in an alcoholic stupor, he's succumbed to undiagnosed liver disease. He's fucking *drunk* himself to death.

The clock seems to move forward so slowly, but at last we're putting up the 'Closed' sign and I'm saying goodbye to Isha on the front step. I've arranged to meet Balkar at the Old Swan at half eight. If I don't talk to someone about it, I'm going to explode and leave a sticky mess and turban remnants all over the shop floor. Balkar's my oldest mate; maybe not the greatest choice in Sikhdom for moral advice as he's always been a bit fly, but then again, if I'm genuinely seeking advice and guidance, why haven't I planned a meeting with the elders at the Gurdwara?

I leave the shop having just added *lying to the wife* to my burgeoning list of prohibitive Sikh behaviour: I told her that Balkar has an interesting business proposition for me and that there's potentially a lot of money to be had. I get there at twenty to nine. I can see his muscular frame stuck behind a pint of Ma Pardoe's best bitter at a nearby table. He's the same age as me, a stone lighter and he's looking a million dollars in a white tee-shirt that shows off his torso and brown biceps. The joys of the singleton. Balkar's a ladies' man and lately he's been playing the field.

"How are things?" I enquire.

"Get us a pint in before I tell you my life story. What kept you? There's been quality drinking time going to waste."

"Doesn't seem to have held you back," I remark as I turn towards the bar.

Am I really going to tell Balkar? What the hell am I thinking of, anyway? I *have* to give back the ticket the next time the bloke walks into the shop. No crime's been committed – I simply say that I put the ticket aside, then noticed the numbers as I was about to bin it. I'm now informing him of his good fortune. Very public spirited. Maybe he'll offer me a nice fat reward?

As for Balkar, we've gone our separate ways. In our teenaged years he was the class shy-guy with zero self-esteem. One summer, I found that his problem was dyslexia. As I was feted as the Brown Bard, I sat with him day after day in the holidays and we worked our way through dozens of American comics. He went back to school in the September reading really well. He's never forgotten my part in that and it formed a bond. These days, he's what you'd call a loveable rogue, I suppose,

41

always dodgy dealing: videos, watches, hi-fi, etc. Everybody buys from him and asks no questions. Shameful really. Jas used to have a soft spot for him. He was the first of my mates that she met as a young bride, fresh off the plane. He seemed quite settled at the time, with a girl that everyone expected him to marry. Jas liked his cheek; she'd never met anyone remotely like him back in the Punjab. She was less impressed a couple of years ago, when he dropped the long-term fiancée and began to play the field again. Since then, I've seen him for the odd pint but we don't really socialise these days.

"Are you planning on ordering, or just looking ornamental?" asks the barmaid. I look for humour, there's none; she's bored, tired, sweaty and impatient.

"Is it the blue turban you're in love with?" I enquire.

Her look says that it most decidedly isn't.

I return to the table with two pints of bitter. In spite of the barmaid, the description: 'a pint of bitter' does no justice to Ma Pardoe's beer – it's the nectar of the Gods, a living, brown, effervescent soupçon of Paradise that has a justified place of honour in the proud history of Black Country ales. I feel proud of that description. I might just send it to the brewery. If there was true justice in the world, they'd award me with a beer pump of my own with Ma Pardoe's permanently on tap.

"You all right, Rakki? I thought you'd gone into a trance over there," says Balkar.

"Lot on my mind. Don't *you* start, I've just had a gob-full from the barmaid."

"She's a mouthy mare, that one. Anyway, what's all this cloak and dagger stuff? I haven't been able to drag you out for a pint in fucking ages, then over the phone you make it sound like life and death?"

"Did it sound that desperate?"

"Like it was a real big deal."

I'm still nervous, unsure whether this is such a good idea. Finally, I come to a decision. "Look, if Jas ever asks: this was a *business* meeting. You've been dabbling into something honest for a change, the potential is huge and you wondered whether I was interested in coming in. Have you got that?"

"Honest for a change! Cheeky bastard!"

"A *business* meeting, Balkar."

He's puzzled. "Seems a bit extreme for a one night pass-out? I hope that Rakki hasn't lost control of his woman?"

"Money's very tight, we've cut spending to the bone and I'm laying down all sorts of economic restrictions. It's the only way I can justify coming out for a beer."

"Poor sod! Bloody hell, things *must* be bad. You should never have left the Post Office, old mate."

"I wish … anyway, I am where I am."

"You're not seriously telling me that we have to justify a pint to Jas though, are you?"

"That's about the size of it."

He shakes his head by way of commiseration. "So, what's the big deal? I'm intrigued."

I had the entire speech planned. Now, I just don't know where to start. "Look, mate, this has to be in the strictest confidence – promise?"

"I *promise,* for Fuck's sake!"

43

"OK, this is hypothetical: What would you do if you found a winning lottery ticket, with say, four point six million riding on it?"

Balkar relaxes, sits back, grins like a Cheshire cat. "What would I do? I'd have the biggest week-long piss-up that Dudley's ever seen! I'd have two huge illuminated plastic fingers made in a 'V' shape and I'd walk around the foundry sticking 'em up the noses of every boss in sight. I'd get laid by every blonde under twenty-one, between here and the Birmingham Bull Ring. I'd buy me a shiny black Beamer, fresh off the production line. I'd have a penthouse flat in the middle of Birmingham's night life, complete with leather, reclining shagging settees. What do you *mean*, what would I do with four and a half million, you dick-head?"

Stupid question, entirely predictable answer, I could have written it down in advance. So what *am* I here for? To get Balkar's blessing for a criminal act?

Balkar senses the atmosphere and the smile drops from his face. "You're having a laugh, right? You said 'hypothetical' – you haven't really found a ticket worth four and a half million?"

"Not exactly *found;* it belongs to a down and out who uses the shop. Last Sunday, as I was checking it, he was rude to Jas, and she chucked him out. He left it behind."

"Good for Jas! She's got some balls, your missus. Serves him right. So does he know it's a winner?"

"Doubtful if he even remembers giving it to me – he was badly hung-over. Most of the time he doesn't even know what day of the week it is."

"So, what's the plan?"

"I guess I'll give it back." I don't sound very convincing, not even to myself.

"Now, you've *got* to be joking? Finders keepers! Anyway, what's a guy like that ever going to do with millions? He'd be ripped off twenty-four/seven. Six months from now, he'd be found dead under a pile of empties."

"I've been there already, telling myself I'd be doing him a favour, saving him from himself, etc. We both know that's bollocks."

"You'd know how to spend it, that's all I'm saying."

"It's so bloody tempting. We're not just poor, we're in financial trouble."

"Like what?"

"It started when they pulled down the flats – I lost more than half my customer-base. Takings are at rock bottom, debts are piling up, some loans are due to be called in any day soon. You name it."

"What more encouragement d'you need? Lady Luck's stepped in and waved her magic wand!"

"But it would be totally dishonest, just plain theft."

"Think, Rakki. Whatever you say to the contrary, there are countless tales of people like him coming into money and ending tragically. One bloke was found dead in his new luxury flat surrounded by piles of booze. He'd been lying there for over six months. You'd be doing this guy a favour. If your conscience is that delicate, open a few charities, spread the gravy around, look after your mates!" He grins. "Only joking!"

"I dunno. I need to think."

"Believe me, if the silly sod hasn't put his name on it, then the ticket's yours, mate. Nobody can say different. I take it, you've not told Jas?"

"You've got to be joking?"

"Cash it, man! If it was me, I'd have been in London, camped outside Camelot first thing on Monday morning."

"I'm not you."

"Why come and bend my ears, then?"

We both know I've no answer to that one.

3

We tell no one. Leave home with a *Closed until Further Notice* sign on the shop. Head for London with the ticket. Jas is still half in denial, she tries to drag me back from the doorway of the Savoy Hotel. She's ecstatic, terrified, excited. How can such an amazing thing have happened? How can we possibly afford the price of a hotel like this? But our credit-worthiness is gainsaid by the lottery ticket: six golden numbers. We meet next morning with a winners' advisor from Camelot and Jas is finally convinced. Instantly, we are given the full VIP treatment. Nothing is too much trouble for the winners' advisory team. We return for a validation meeting, our heads spinning, our feet not touching the ground. They arrange a meeting with a representative from a private bank, to find a temporary home for our fortune. They want to know if we want to go public... *No! We certainly do not!* Jas is somewhat taken aback by the strength of my reply, but the Camelot team take it very much in their stride. Between meetings, we wander the capital in a dream-like state, showing the kids the sights. They advise us to take a short holiday to let the win sink in – Jas, could not agree more, she has but one thought in her mind – to untangle us from this whirlwind and catch the first plane to India to share the good news with her Mum and family.

Visas are no problem – special arrangements are made and the Indian Embassy deliver within three days.

We check out of the Savoy on the fourth day. Air tickets and travel arrangements all fell smoothly into place and we are taking a private-hire limousine to Heathrow. I'm learning quickly that nothing is too much trouble for the nouveau riche. And what have I done to earn it? I've nicked some poor devil's lottery ticket. Would I be any more deserving of such sycophancy if I'd hit upon the six random numbers myself? I think not. I'm beginning to understand: the plain simple truth is that people are dazzled by the rich and award them a natural deference. It's not even about any hope on their part of personal gain, they're just bending to the natural order of things. I wonder whether I'm ever going to get used to it.

There are very few people in the Concorde Room – the exclusive space that British Airways reserve for people such as ourselves. Our lives are becoming more rarefied by the hour. We're ushered into a first class suite in the Boeing 747 and find ourselves surrounded by sheer unadulterated luxury. We're sitting in seats big enough for two. Within five minutes, we're eating canapés, I'm sipping champagne and Jas has opted for freshly pressed fruit juice. The kids settle down to watch TV: they're drinking huge glasses of iced Coke whilst Jas and I idle over the extensive on-board menu. There's no particular hurry – I'm assured that it's instantly available at all hours throughout the flight.

I sit, remembering the only other time I flew to India – the match-making mission. I was in tourist class, of course. I recall trying to drink tea with the elbow of a stale, snoring stranger buried deep into my side, whilst the bastard in front reclined his seat to rob me of my only remaining personal space. My God, it's *all* about money. How the other half live! The penny drops again: I *am* the other half now. I'm living the dream.

Jas has adapted quickly. She's been ecstatic, ever since the official confirmation. It's as though she's been waiting all her life for this moment. How long is it since she looked like that? Those are the eyes I saw on the first day we met. Sangi's happy because her mum and dad are happy and Amal is Amal, although even that's not strictly true: he seemed fascinated by the plane and since one of the hostesses gave him an aircraft book, he's not taken his eyes from the pages. I buy into Jas' infectious mood and begin to entertain them with stories about the shop.

"Remember the chocolate rep' who told you how sad he was I'd died?" I ask her.

Jas chuckles.

"Why, Daddy?" asks Sangi, with a worried look.

"He'd been to McKenzie's sweet shop down the road – you know, Mr McKenzie, the guy with the thick Glasgow accent? When he asked where Basra's Stores was, Mackenzie told him, 'He's just diagonally opposite.'"

"So why did he think you were dead?"

"Because he'd heard, 'He's just died in the office'. Poor guy. He was in the middle of offering your mum his commiserations when I walked through. It was him that almost died – of embarrassment."

Sangi didn't like that one, but the memory brought a smile to Jas' lips.

"When we get back, I'm going to buy you a Stradivarius," I tell my daughter.

"Well that's going to take all of your money then, Daddy, they cost millions."

"No – there are cheap ones."

"They're *millions,* Dad."

"That can't be right – otherwise why would they call them Stradi Various?"

"Dad!"

It was a crap joke. The family are well used to suffering my awful puns. In her present mood, Jas is ready to laugh at anything, but I can see a little hurt in Sangi's eyes.

"No, seriously Sangi – it might not be a Strad', but when we get back to London, we're going shopping at the best music shop we can find! You'll be getting the violin of your dreams."

Jas and the kids watch a film. It's a latest release fantasy film full of gremlin-like creatures and flying dragons – not my cup of tea at all, but Jas is almost as enthusiastic as the children. I stretch my legs and get chatting to a fellow first-classer. He's the director of a large charity that runs a number of NGOs across India. It makes me wonder what he's doing at my end of the aircraft, but who am I to cast the first stone?

He's an interesting guy. He talks about India being a booming, emerging nation. A young country despite its ancient roots. A land full of idealistic kids bursting for learning. Kids who know that education is the way out of poverty, to a desirable lifestyle. I tell him about some of my former young Netherton customers – the beer-swilling lager louts, who sleep through eleven years of free education and leave school unable to put together intelligent sentences. I'm not sure that he altogether believes me. It pauses him only briefly and he goes on to describe some of his pioneering work setting up centres in remote villages, curing the sick, educating the poor and teaching them skills. It makes me wonder whether it's something that I could consider doing in the future, but wisely, I keep my own counsel. I learn that by some miracle, India is the world's biggest democracy and that against all odds, it holds genuine elections in twenty-eight federal states for its one and a quarter billion inhabitants. Its people speak over two hundred and sixteen languages and ten of the states have a population larger than Great Britain. I feel humbled, inspired and more aware than ever that I've lived my life in almost total ignorance of my ancestral homeland.

Later, somewhere over Turkmenistan, when the rarefied few around us are safely asleep, surreptitiously, Jas and I join the Mile High Club via our adjoining seat beds. It's almost impossible to imagine that we're flying in an aluminium tube, thousands of feet above the Earth's surface. Deep in the darker recesses of my mind, I know the Mile High ambition has always been there – and who better to share it with than the love of my life? The tired, depressed partner of recent years has vanished and I'm lying beside the ardent young bride I married almost twenty years ago.

India's a shock to the system. It's a truism, but no less a fact for that. My chat with the charity director has done nothing to mitigate first contact. The heat, the crowds, the pollution, the overt poverty, the dazzling assortment of multi-coloured humanity, the noise, the smells: the mind has to adjust to so many differing impressions. The same obsequiousness we've experienced in London and on the plane extends to New Delhi Airport and onwards to our multi-star greeting at the five star Golden Temple Hotel. If we thought we had been given *la crème de la crème* treatment in GB, here in India, it's *la crème de la crème de la crème*. It doesn't sit any easier on me than it did back there. Sangi explores our luxury suite excitedly, Amal sits and gapes at the wall to wall TV. Jas takes immediate advantage of the capacious bathroom, she wants to try the hot-tub, the multi-jet shower, the soaps, the creams and the perfumes. I tell Sangi I'm going for a stroll outside.

On the street, the air hits me again like a furnace. No wonder we Sikhs were so well-suited to the sweat and toil of the African railways and GB's foundries! This must be the flip-side of town, New Delhi's underbelly. A pack of debilitated, mangy street dogs stand sentinel around a dead comrade, not fifty feet from the hotel entrance. I think *rabies,* but nobody seems to be giving them a second glance. Ragged kids are on my case the second my sandals contact the pavement. They hold out their hands and give me their most winsome smiles. I ignore them, knowing that any reward will bring a blitz of others down upon me. I pick my way through the waiting tuk-tuks and narrowly miss being flattened by a speeding, colourful lorry, all but obliterated by its headlamps. The driver is a grinning homicidal maniac, clearly blinded by the glittering chrome accoutrements.

Half a street on, the hotel gives way to pavement dwellers, half-hidden under hard-won bits of tarpaulin and rusty sheets of corrugated iron. A street food-seller is cooking-up over a portable gas ring in what looks to be a metal dustbin lid. He's doing a lively trade. Hot portions from the lid are spooned into flatbread and deftly wrapped by his conscientious assistant, a sliver of a girl no older than eight. They both look in urgent need of a bellyful of their own medicine. The price is ten rupees: in the hotel, that kind of small change wouldn't get you an ice cube for your drink. Three teenaged lads are standing right next to them, pouring soapy water over each other's skinny torsos from a cracked plastic bucket –wash, brush-up and evening meal, Delhi street-style. Dusky faces peer out from rickety shelters: some raise a palm, more in habit than hope. An elderly guy with a crude, plastic false left hand sits cross-legged, next to an empty begging dish and a pile of metal. I take a closer look at the pile of scrap and find that it's an ancient, rust-ridden Avery weighing machine. The machine last functioned with any vestige of accuracy probably at some time during the British Raj, but there are no takers anyway. His travail is about as heroic as selling ice cream to Eskimos. It's unthinkable that half-starved slum-dwellers would ever perceive the need to weigh themselves. I choose my moment and drop him a quick one hundred rupee note. He tries to grasp my ankle, chanting his gratitude. He can feast on street food for the next ten days with that. *Shit,* he would have needed five *fashionistas* on his scales just to have earned tonight's supper.

The street overflows with a moving tide of humanity. Most of India is on parade: old hags and gurus, bare-bummed babies playing in the roadside dirt, toddlers no bigger than sixpence, youngsters apprenticed already to a dozen street trades, pedlars and beggars of all shapes, ages and sizes. Svelte young beauties glide by in bright saris, unmarked as yet by the hazards of pavement childbirth and the disease, deformity and poverty of their mothers. Tatty tuk-tuks tangle with dazzling psychedelic taxis and austere-looking small-windowed buses chase by, crammed to bursting point with fares. And everywhere, smiling faces: street food sellers, bead sellers, knife grinders, postcard and trinket touts beckoning and grinning through their milk-white teeth. They know me for a tourist, despite my brown face. They smile through their adversity in a manner unknown to the mean streets of London. Suddenly I take fright lest my ill-gotten wealth should strike me down and put me amongst them. I hurry back to my hotel.

I had a similar deep-seated fear on my first trip. I felt alien. I'm *of* this land, but not part of it. I'm reminded of those grainy photos of nineteen sixties Brits on the Costa Brava. I'm one of them now, with their baggy shorts and knobbly, white knees and their hankies knotted on their heads: a Brit abroad, slightly ridiculous, out of sorts and out of his depth. A stranger in my own land. I take the express lift back to the penthouse suite, sweating and trembling, grateful and guilty for the insulation of *having* in a land of have-nots.

Jas is waiting for me with fear in her eyes. "Why the hell did you do that?" she demands.

"What?"

"*Disappear* like that?"

I'm taken aback by the strength of her reaction. "What's the problem? I told Sangi I was going. Big mistake, as it turns out – it's forty-one centigrade out there!"

I grin ruefully. It's not returned.

"This is bloody *Delhi*, Rakesh. Can't you try and remember that?"

"Oh, come on Jas! You're not suggesting -"

"Thirty years is *nothing!*" she snaps. "Save your walkabouts for Majitha."

I nod sheepishly. I may not be from around here, but everybody's heard of the anti-Sikh riots in Delhi. I think it was 1984. Thousands of Sikhs were murdered and more recently it's been renamed *The Sikh Genocide*. Jas has scared me. It was a long time ago – but she has local knowledge. I know only that it's commemorated in London every year, when Sikhs march through the capital. I'm embarrassed that I've never taken the trouble to get my head around the event and I'm *not* about to show my ignorance: I was a thirteen year-old kid at the time, for God's sake – and four thousand miles away!

I try to look casual and tell her I'll be more careful about going out. Secretly, I feel a renewed determination to discover more about my heritage.

Next day, we catch a connecting flight to Amritsar. Amritsar, the site of Harmandir Sahib, the holiest of our Gurdwaras – better known in the west as The Golden Temple. To us, it's St Peter's in Rome, St Paul's Cathedral, the Temple on the Mount, the Kaaba of Mecca – all rolled into one. Every Sikh should go there at least once in his lifetime. I visited briefly when I was on my wife-hunting safari and now try to forgive myself for having been so casual about it. This trip, I'm determined to give it more attention and to make sure that Sangita and Amal do, too.

We're staying at the five-star Hyatt Amritsar. From there, it will be just a daily eighteen kilometre car ride to Jas's family in Majitha. We won't stay with them, of course, a Sikh doesn't stay under the roof of his wife's family. We'll visit each day. The Hyatt stands out in contrast to its pitiful surroundings in the same way as the Golden Temple Hotel did in New Delhi. Jas can't wait to try out the spa and its eight treatment rooms. First priority, however, is to hire a driver and to give her mum and old uncle the good news. As yet, no one knows we're in town. For us, everything is possible – the word 'difficult' has disappeared from our dictionary. *I* don't have to hire a driver, or to worry about which firm is best value – I simply pass the issue on to the hotel reception, knowing that they were born to do my bidding.

I'm still trying to ponder the enigma of my ancestral homeland. When we Sikhs abandoned the caste system and named all of our kin equal with the ubiquitous 'Singh' and 'Kaur', it was to acknowledge the end of hierarchy. But here in the Punjab, like everywhere the world over, hierarchy is alive and well. Maybe it's ingrained in the remaining belief we share with the Hindus: in the stepped nature of the progression of the soul on its journey through many existences to the final fusion with God. If the poor, the hungry, the sick and the needy are where they should be on that personal soul journey, then – no matter how contrary to Sikh beliefs of equality – is it any wonder that fellow travellers seem indifferent to their fate?

India is a land where one in five live in poverty and where corruption still reigns supreme. My friend on the plane mentioned a report in *Transparency International* that describes fifty-six per cent of the population having encountered corruption in their daily lives and an annual loss to national development of *fifty billion US dollars!* I've heard anecdotally that you're lucky to get a telephone connected, or your electricity turned on, without pushing rupee notes under the counter. It's a land that has spawned a thousand new millionaires in ten years and most of them do their best to pay little or no taxes. A land where even today, if your name's not right you can be excluded from a job. The caste system's dead, but long live the caste system! All Sikhs are born equal, but long live hierarchy!

Jas shares none of my angst. In spite of the huge elevation in her circumstances, as soon as we reach Majitha she's fully at home. We arrive in some style and within half an hour, we're the talk of the neighbourhood. The locals all seem to believe that we're visiting millionaires – but *shit!* – we *are!* And Jas has no problem with shouting it from the rooftops. Her mum's brothers and sisters, nephews, nieces and cousins flock to the family house that she shares with Uncle Gurdip. It's a modest dwelling: two stories and a little smallholding, but up-market by local comparison. Jas's granddad, her dad and after his death, her uncle Gurdip, all sold their vegetables at market. No matter how poor they were, no one starved. Her mum is fond of saying that they're related to one of Maharaja Ranjit Singh's generals – an ancestor whom the Maharaja recruited into his famous Sikh army.

For ten days, we shuttle backwards and forwards from our hotel in our shiny, black limousine with the uniformed driver who never once deigns to speak with the peasants of Majitha. Jas's days are filled with exciting missions to exclusive air-conditioned shopping malls – commercial wonderlands, sanitised of the inconvenience of beggars and unfortunates by their monitored entrances. Money worries have scattered like feathers on a breeze: Jas's mother will get her eye operation under the best specialist in Amritsar, a builder has been engaged to improve and extend the family home, the numerous children of the family will never need to worry again about the money to attend school.

When we're in Majitha, Grandma takes the lion's share of looking after Amal. He seems quite content, as far as one can tell. Jas has decided already that the future English property must have a granny flat – she sees her mother shuttling backwards and forwards to help out. I can't see it happening; as far as I know, the old lady has never been further than Amritsar. Sangita's Punjabi is very stilted but she's found a friend in Harneet, one of her distant cousins. They never stop talking. This afternoon they're off to see a Bollywood movie with Harneet's brother Arjan, riding shotgun. The girls of the family are not allowed out alone – Sangi finds this very insulting, but privately her mother and I are relieved.

One afternoon, when the rest of them are on a 'shop 'til you drop', I'm left alone with old Uncle Gurdip. He's the doyen of the family and reputed to be seventy-seven – ten years older than Jas's father would have been had he lived. It's the opportunity I've been looking for, a chance to discover more about the Sikh Genocide. He must have been in his forties at the time.

It's clear that he finds me a pretty strange kind of a Sikh – not yet a member of the Khalsa – speaking Punjabi with what probably sounds like a Black Country accent, completely anglicised, ill-at-ease in my traditional homeland and ignorant of so much of my historical roots. After a few opening verbal skirmishes, he takes pity on me.

"So, where do you want me to start?"

We talk all afternoon. His memory is crystal clear and his knowledge surprisingly wide-ranging. By the time the others come home full of fun and excitement and loaded with goodies that were far out of reach only days ago, I've had a full history lesson. I've gained the deepest respect for him and all that he has suffered. I'm a sadder and hopefully, a wiser man and I'm more confused about my identity than ever before.

Jas wants to spend the early evening in the opulence of the hotel's spa. We awaken the dozing chauffeur and he drives the two of us back to Amritsar. Between us we sample most of the expensive treatments available to two such wealthy, deserving people. Jas is looking vibrant and beautiful and positively glows with health and well-being. The spa, the dramatically changed circumstances, the warm, heady nights, the spicy food of our forefathers, all of these things have given back to her a libido that since the birth of Amal has been at best, spasmodic and stunted. In the luxury of our hotel suite she is overtaken by an urgency I've not witnessed since the earliest days of our relationship; a heat and a passion that in Dudley, I could never have imagined would return.

I lie beside her, unable to raise my manhood and overwhelmed with shame.

"Don't worry," she tells me, "so many changes. You'll be fine once we get our dream house back home." We cuddle like friends caught out in a storm and I wonder if she's conscious of the disappointment in her voice.

Once we get our dream house back home... Is that what I want? My conscience is beginning to wear me down. In a hostel in England, there's a guy trying to put the money together for his next few cans of cider, a man who rightfully has the wealth to buy up the orchards and the entire bloody brewery. Here, thousands of my father's generation died for the crime of being Sikhs. I grew up free and easy, footballing and eyeing the girls in a land more tolerant than I ever knew. I've made my bed and I must lie in it. There'll be a beautiful house for the kids to grow up in and to flourish. There'll be additional specialised help for little Amal and a new violin and extra tuition for my lovely Sangita. We can stop worrying about their futures. Jas will be happy and fulfilled: new house, new car, new friends, new pursuits. There'll be no failing grocery store, no debts around our necks, no burning of the midnight oil to paper over the financial cracks and no time spent robbing Peter to pay Paul.

I guess I've just got to get used to it all.

4

We take our time showering and dressing and then enter one of the express lifts for the hotel's restaurant complex. We have the choice of European, Chinese or Indian and to please Jas, I suggest Indian.

I let Jas do the ordering: after all, she's the local expert. The austere-looking Sikh who serves us does his best to hide his disdain. I choose a delicate array of tiny hot meat starters lying on a bed of finely shredded onions. I'm half way through them when the first wave of heat hits me. I say nothing and reach for the chilled champagne. Jas notices anyway and enquires if I'm all right.

She smiles. "They're not *that* hot, Rakki! You've no stomach for good Indian food, have you?"

By now, I've a blinding pain that's set up behind the eyes.

"Jas, I'm ill," I tell her. "I've got to get out of here."

I see her look of amusement change swiftly to one of concern and the fear in her eyes sets my heart banging fiercely. I rise and with her support, I stagger towards the lifts, desperate now to escape the inquisitive stares of other diners, lest their looks turn fearful and hostile. I hold out until Jas gets the door open to our suite, but I can't make it into the palatial bathroom. I cover the carpet in vomit and as I retch I'm losing control of the other end too.

"Oh my God! Oh my God!" Jas is muttering as she tries her best to support me over the toilet. "We need a doctor, Rakki. Let's see if I can sit you down, whilst I call Reception?" Somehow she removes my trousers and underpants as I grip the bowl.

"Don't bring anyone in to see me – not in this state," I groan.

She manoeuvres me into the empty bathtub and after ensuring that my head can reach the toilet bowl, ignoring my pleas, she runs back into the bedroom to summon help.

The fever, the sickness and the diarrhoea stop as suddenly as they started. I'm shivering now, shaking from head to foot. Jas returns and peels me out of the rest of my soiled clothes.

"They're sending a doctor," she says. "Everything will be all right."

I sit there in the tub, weak and disorientated, with my teeth chattering uncontrollably, whilst my redoubtable wife gently hoses me down with warm water to remove the soiling. I'm too ill to care now, helpless like an infant during nappy change.

A doctor arrives. I've lost track of time – we might have been waiting ten minutes, or it might have been an hour or more. He's talking urgently with Jas. I'm burning again and the headache's almost intolerable. She dabs my forehead with a wet towel and tells me that I'm going to hospital.

"It could be gastroenteritis, Rakki, but the doctor thinks that either malaria or dengue fever is more likely. I told him that you were badly bitten by mosquitoes that first night in Delhi."

"How bad is that?" I croak.

The doctor intervenes. "With rapid, effective treatment, Mr Basra, you should be all right in ten days or so. The important thing is to get you to a hospital for the correct diagnosis and treatment."

Jas is crying and it unnerves me. "D'you think I'm going to die?" I mutter.

The doctor takes over again. "The ambulance will be here directly, Mr Basra. We shall be taking you to the finest private hospital in Amritsar."

Jas is with me in the ambulance. I'm lapsing in and out of consciousness. Behind my eyes my brain feels as if it's being ripped apart. I'm shivering and sweating, not even sure whether I'm feeling boiling hot or freezing cold.

I'm in a bed now. It must be hospital – there's a drip fixed into my arm. The shakes and the fever go up and down as before and I'm feeling so ill. Is it the same night, or has some time gone by? Jas is beside me, talking to me. I make a big effort to focus.

"Can you hear me, Rakki? You're going to be all right. It's dengue fever. Thankfully, the doctors don't think it's the haemorrhagic type. You're going to feel really poorly for a few days, but they've told me you will get better quite quickly afterwards. You'll probably come out in a big rash. Try not to worry now. you have this lovely room all to yourself and I can stay close by you."

I nod weakly to indicate that I've understood. It's difficult to believe that I'm going to get better. Maybe they're lying to allay my worries? In spite of my doubts, some small part of me registers relief that someone is saying that death won't claim me.

I close my eyes and feel the warmth of my wife's hand in mine. I love her and I will never let go. The fever is upon me again.

I'm Gurdip, I'm ten years old and I'm fleeing with my family into the night, away from our village of Kalibair and the murdering Pakistanis. My dad has been angry for weeks. He refused to believe that the British would give us away to the new land of Pakistan, but they *have*. I've listened to him and his friends and I've tried to understand. We live near to the holy city of Nankana Sahib, the birthplace of our prophet, Guru Nanak. Less than one hundred miles away to the west, beyond the city of Lahore, lies Amritsar and Harmandir Sahib, our greatest Gurdwara. Dad says that all of the Punjab should be ours, in a land called Khalistan, where our holy city and our holy temple would be united. And now the British have done the worst thing that anyone could ever imagine: they have created the new land of Pakistan and put the border with India on the other side of Lahore, dividing Nankana Sahib and Harmandir Sahib forever.

So now we live in the new land of Pakistan. There's no more time for anger; the Moslems are burning our villages and hunting down Hindus and Sikhs like vermin. We have only water and dried chapattis and the clothes in which we stand and Dad has instructed Mum and me on what we must do: we have to hide in creeks and bushes during the day and follow the setting sun towards Amritsar and freedom beyond the new border. If we are discovered, he will run and take his chances, so that they may be drawn away from us. I don't like the plan, but he says that there will be no mercy if they catch us and it is better that two escape than none at all.

We walk until I am exhausted, but I will never complain. Sometimes we see other figures in the night. Everyone is running towards Lahore, but Dad says that we must take time and go around it. The city is in the hands of bloodthirsty Moslems and we would be set on fire or dangled from the trees. As the horizon becomes grey before the first rays of the sun, Dad finally calls a halt. We find a cutting that he thinks is a dried watercourse that will lead to the Ravi River. Tonight we must cross the Ravi, but for now we pull branches and leaves over ourselves and hide as best we can. My mother is crying softly; her belly is big and painful with the new baby that she carries and she fears that she cannot go on. In spite of the terror in my chest I can no longer keep open my eyes.

It's very confusing. I'm Rakki again and Jas is bathing my forehead with an ice cool flannel. I feel so very, very ill. In spite of what they say, I'm sure I'm going to die in this hospital bed and my heart fills with regrets. I try to talk but only a weak croaking sound emerges, prompting Jas to shush me and reassure me that I'm going to be all right. My meeting with old Uncle Gurdip is at the forefront of my mind and I'm sure that I've dreamed of him, too. I want to recover and live to be a better Sikh and to put right the terrible crime that I've committed. If I'm spared I'll find a way.

Darkness has fallen and Dad thinks it's safe to move. We follow the dried creek and trip and bruise our legs and feet in the darkness. I'm eaten alive by mosquitoes and I try not to scratch or think of the pain. Mum asks whether we

65

can climb out of the ditch and follow its bank and Dad thinks it's now safe enough to try. A half moon is lighting our way, making the going easier but more hazardous. Up ahead we hear weird animal-like howling and Dad orders us to drop to our knees and to crawl forward slowly. My poor mother obeys and grits her teeth as her belly scrapes along the rough ground. The howling stops, but my father calls a halt and we wait a while until he feels that it's all right to continue.

We stumble into a clearing and I fall heavily. I turn to see what blocked my way and look directly into the eyes of a dead man. The blood around his turban is fresh and still dripping to the ground. My Dad urges me forward and tells me not to look, but I do. We are surrounded by the dead; men, women, children and even a small baby. They are Sikhs like ourselves and their heads and teeth and eyes have been smashed with heavy sticks that now lie scattered beside them. Why would anyone want to do such a terrible thing? Why should we be hated so much? Is it just because the British have built a new border? I stay silent all night, even when my father orders me to hold on to him and my mother as we wade out into the waters of the Ravi.

Filthy from the river mud and half-drowned, we crawl on our bellies and eventually find another hole to sleep the day away. Dad tries to comfort us with soothing words: soon we will be in Amritsar, among our own people in the land of India. We have water to drink and our bellies will just have to wait for food. What a feast we will have when we reach Harmandir Sahib and seek charity within the kitchens of its holy interior! My dad says that thousands are fed within its precincts every single day. I can't imagine anything so big.

On the fifth night of our flight, Dad feels sure that we've crossed the line of the new border. There is nothing to say what is India and what is Pakistan – can such an imaginary line have caused so many people to run and to die? As dawn breaks we walk out of the fields to the first village we encounter. Mum and I lie low as Dad crawls forward to make sure that he is not mistaken and he returns smiling with a group of our own people. The women help my poor mother to her feet and later that morning, she gives birth to my little brother.

We remain in the village for ten days, until my mother is fit enough to continue the journey to Amritsar. My father isn't sure where we will seek out a new home, but before all else, he wants to offer his thanks inside the great walls and golden towers of Harmandir Sahib. The village that has shown us such kindness has filled with dozens of others who have fled the new Pakistan. Everywhere, they are greeted with friendship and a willingness by the people to share what little they have.

Frequently, I hear men talking excitedly about how many Moslems they have caught and killed fleeing in the other direction and my father participates in the celebrations. For the first time, I realise that the new border has brought death and disaster to people living on both sides. I try not to hate the Moslems – they were my friends at school, we played together and we lived side by side in the same streets. But now I suppose that if they want to kill us, we must kill them first. Does it mean that our two new countries are going to start a war? Nobody seems to know. Some say that when everyone has run away to where they are supposed to be, everything will settle down.

I wake again and I'm shaking so hard that I fear my bones will break. A red light is flashing above me and people in white coats float by. Somewhere in the middle, I can make out Jas' face, taut, grey and fearful. I'm past caring now, I just want the sickness to leave me even if death has to take me. Someone is injecting my arm and I feel the tremors begin to subside.

"So are you with us, Gurdip?"

I'm no longer a small boy of ten – one of the two and half million Sikhs, Hindus and Moslems trapped on the wrong side of the new borders of Partition – I'm a middle-aged man who maybe should know better. We are standing outside the front door of my father's smallholding and I look around at the anxious, questioning eyes of my neighbours. Men I grew up with here in Majitha, farmers, shopkeepers, industrial and agricultural labourers. Peaceable, hardworking people, now armed and angry, driven by Indira Ghandi and her high-handed Congress Party to consider desperate measures.

"How can a man stand idly by when there is talk of an attack upon Harmandir Sahib itself?" demands a second voice.

How can it have come to this? We tried the democratic route: asked under the Anandpur Resolution for special recognition and an autonomous homeland. We saw it as our *right*, for once we ruled *all* of the Punjab. The request was met by arrests and imprisonment for all who would agitate for a Sikh homeland! I've been a man of peace all of my life but the ratchet turns a little tighter each day. Since nineteen seventy five we've been in an official state of internal emergency and more recently, Ghandi declared that she would govern the Punjab by President's Rule – directly, dictatorially.

"I'm with you," I tell them.

I am my father's son and I will *not* fall timidly under the heel of an oppressor. Since the long flight of nineteen forty-seven, my parents brought up my brother and me to be good citizens of India. But is this India, when the government treats us like criminals in our own land? Few of us had much time for Jarnail Singh Bhindranwale and his militant hotheads when first they began their armed insurgency, but now they've taken refuge in our holy Gurdwara and Ghandi is threatening to lay siege to the temple itself!

The stand-off has been going on for weeks whilst the police, the army and the politicians discussed what to do. Now, it seems that Ghandi has made up her mind. Yesterday, June the third, she placed the Punjab under curfew. Complete censorship has been imposed, all foreign journalists have been kicked out and everybody knows that a showdown is on the way. This government will not be allowed to desecrate Harmandir Sahib. We'll give Bhindranwale what help we can.

We wait until nightfall and make our way over the fields towards Amritsar and our holy temple. As we draw close, towards dawn, we hear the boom of field artillery echoing out across the summer landscape. We cross a village close to Harmandir Sahib and find women wailing over their dead. Several houses have been razed by shells and we are told that the men fought bravely against overwhelming army numbers and were quickly despatched. My heart hardens with resolve, but it's difficult to imagine how eighteen men with one pistol between them and a variety of knives, sticks and farm implements can face the might of a modern army.

We crawl to within sight of our Gurdwara and a horrific sight befalls us: Harmandir Sahib has been shelled with field guns and large sections of its outer walls lie in ruins. Men in Indian Army uniform are dragging corpses down the main steps and piling them on the ground. Bhindranwale's freedom fighters have been defeated and judging by the growing pile of bodies, all five hundred have met their end.

We are a bunch of unarmed peasants, there's not a fighting man amongst us and with the exception of Dalbir Singh Gupta, we're all well past our youth. It's a bitter pill to swallow, had we been here sooner, I would have entered Harmandir Sahib unthinkingly and defended its walls with my life.

"To attack now would be suicide," I tell my comrades. "We're too late!"

Just upon it, a group of sappers emerges from Harmandir Sahib's Eastern gate carrying holy relics and sacred books. The men are shouting and laughing, drunk with the thrill of battle and they begin to scatter the items down the steps.

It is all too much for young Dalbir; he breaks cover before any of us can react and begins to run across the two hundred metres of ground separating us from the soldiers. He is brandishing nothing but a short-handled scythe. His father Mohinder, my friend and nearest neighbour, leaps to his feet and would have followed, had we not wrestled him forcibly to the ground.

"Death to the desecrators of Harmandir Sahib!" screams Dalbir. The soldiers drop their remaining booty and four or five of them raise their rifles. As we continue to struggle with Mohinder, half way across the field his son falls in a hail of bullets and lies motionless.

There is nothing more to do but to run and to hope to fight another day. One or two of the soldiers are looking over towards our hiding place, but their curiosity is blunted by the complacency of victory and a kid with a sickle posed no great threat to their safety. It's the bleakest day of my life and as we half-drag, half-carry Mohinder away, we nod and acknowledge to one another that retreat was the only option. Who will help us Sikhs now, when our government is prepared to reject all peaceable demands, to massacre those who would resist and to desecrate our holiest Gurdwara? It sets me wondering whether our fellow citizens are really so different from the Moslems over the border in Pakistan?

As we trudge our weary way home, a voice is calling me by name. It seems to be coming out of the sky itself. 'Gurdip, Gurdip. Rakki, Rakki. Can you hear me?'

I open my eyes and Jas is standing above me.

"You were sobbing, Rakki. Was it a nightmare? How are you feeling?"

I nod weakly.

"The doctor says that the fever has broken. That's a very good sign."

It's true, I'm no longer sweating, or freezing, or shaking, but I find that I have barely the strength to frame a reply.

"Poor Uncle Gurdip," I mutter. "He told me such terrible things."

Jas is looking at me thoughtfully, full of concern. "You were with him on the afternoon before your illness. Has it been on your mind?"

I nod weakly again.

"We have to get you well now, Rakki. No more thinking about all of those terrible things from the past."

I try to smile. My lovely wife needs reassurance that I'm doing my best to get well. I'm not going to reveal the content of my delirious journeying and I feel relief that the Sikh Genocide failed to surface in my nightmares. I shudder involuntarily and hope that the end of the fever means the end of Uncle Gurdip's visitations.

"The rash has started, Rakki – look at your arms." She picks up my right arm and brings it into my line of vision. "It's covered with clusters; the doctor says that's a normal progression. We should have you up and about in a few days time."

She smiles down at me and I manage to elongate my lips.

"Everybody sends you their love, especially Sangi of course. You gave us all such a fright, but in terms of how bad dengue fever can be, they say you've been very, very lucky."

I pull a face. The last thing I'm feeling right now is very, very lucky.

"They're annoyed with us for not having had all of the right jabs before we left Britain, but you don't have to worry – you're full of them now!"

She bends forward and blows me a kiss. "I'm going to leave you for a while, you need to rest and recover. I'll come back in tonight – then tomorrow, Sangi can visit."

I've no idea what time of day it is anyway, but I'm relieved to be left alone, relieved to fall back under the spell of sleep and to hope for dreamless oblivion.

The summer and autumn have passed and I'm filled with bitterness and the gnawing shame and despair of a man who stood by and watched helplessly, as government troops trampled over his soul. I'm no longer fever-Gurdip, I'm dream-Gurdip. I'm Rakesh too, looking on. Such is the flexible logic of dreams. The home movie rolls and I walk through the screen back into the picture. My mind neutralises the twisted logic and I begin to live the next chapter of Gurdip's life from within his skin.

The armed rebellion is over and most Indians think that we Sikhs got what we deserved. I'm back at the brickworks, sweating over the kilns. The talk is quietly subversive, but we've learned what Ghandi and her Congress Party do about dissent. At home there are more pressing issues: my brother Harjeet is mortally ill with lung disease and we are already in premature mourning. It's such a tragic irony: I have no dependents and have spent my life in the heat and the dust of the brickworks. He has a wife and daughter and has always worked in the fresh air of the smallholding, alongside our father. If Fate allowed I'd gladly swap places and take an early cremation. We will rally of course, and I'll take care of his wife Sumitra and little Jasvinder. I shall have to leave the brickworks and work the smallholding. My father is too old and broken now to continue without the input of my brother.

I'm turning the soil in readiness for the winter crops with these thoughts heavy upon my mind when Sumitra comes running across the garden. I fear the worst for Harjeet, but I'm mistaken.

"They've killed Indira Ghandi!" she tells me, breathlessly.

"Who?"

"A group of her Sikh bodyguards, they've shot her!"

"God be praised!" I shout and we begin a little dance around the yard. "At last, Harmandir Sahib and all Sikhs have been avenged! I must run and tell Mohinder. Dalbir did not die in vain!"

Later, we stay close to the radio. India is a country of more than one billion people and it's apparent that few share the joy of the Sikhs. She is being mourned as the Mother of India and already there are demands for reprisals and revenge. The radio is giving free range to opinion: the Sikhs are a festering cancer that should be cut from society! There is no voice of moderation and I begin to fear that a huge black tide will soon roll over the Punjab.

The following day, my worst fears are confirmed. The news from New Delhi is that Sikhs are being hunted down and killed like dogs. In the poorer quarters, houses are torched and entire families thrown back into the flames. Men are hanging from the lampposts, strung up by their turbans with their beards set afire. By nightfall, people running from Amritsar speak of armed gangs abroad, raping and killing at will with the police standing aside to watch.

Harjeet begs me to take his wife and little Jasvinder out into the countryside until the situation is under control. I hide my anger and tell him that I cannot leave him and our elderly parents to the mercy of the mob.

Our father comes to his assistance. "They'll not harm two octogenarians and a dying man!" he insists. He still retains the courage of his youth.

"I can't do it."

My brother turns on me with all of his remaining strength. "Do you want to witness the rape and murder of Jaina and Jasvinder?" he yells, "and then die uselessly for your folly!"

I have no answer and he bids me to hurry and to take provisions and to find shelter where we can, well away from the populated areas.

"Say nothing to us of your plans," he says ominously. "It's better that we know as little as possible."

I have a good friend, a bachelor like myself who left the brickworks to farm a hillside a day's walk away. The farm is isolated and I know that I can depend upon him for food and shelter until the worst is over. I can only hope that vengeance will not spread that far and that the mobs will have had their fill of our blood from the urban areas. We wait for darkness and I do what I can to close my ears to the pleas and wailing of Jaina, as she begs her husband to be allowed to stay with him.

The dream ends and I wake in the half-light of my private hospital suite. I'm shaking and disturbed, but the fever no longer grips me. I'm still half in the mind of poor Gurdip and all that he saw and experienced during those dreadful days. Mercifully, the mob spared his dying brother and their elderly parents and Sumitra and Jasvinder were able to return to say a final farewell.

I press the bedside bell and a nursing assistant appears. I'm well enough for black tea. I lie thinking about all that I now know – of how officials and police were complicit in the massacre of three thousand of my brothers and sisters. How some members of the Congress Party even supplied the mobs with electoral rolls to more effectively hunt down their victims and prominent citizens offered rupee bounties upon the heads of Sikhs. Even Ghandi's son Sanjit was not above the naked revenge: when he flew back from West Bengal and was informed of the massacre, he is reported to have shrugged and commented, 'When a big tree falls, the earth shakes.'

Small wonder that Jas still carries those scars and feared for me, alone upon the streets of New Delhi.

My recovery grows apace and soon I'm strong enough for discharge. It's been a salutary lesson upon the dangers of travelling here without taking appropriate precautions. Not for the first time, I thank God for the elevated status that protects and sets apart even the humblest of western travellers on the Indian sub-continent. My own dirty money puts me upon an altogether different plane – where the entire spectrum of advanced medicine and care is at my disposal, in facilities that have been purpose-built and tailor-made to cater privately for the wealthy sick of the world.

We rest for a few days in the luxury of our hotel until I feel strong enough to revisit Jas' mother and Uncle Gurdip. I treat him now with the respect that he deserves and invite him to accompany us on a visit to Harmandir Sahib – the abode of God. To my delight he agrees. I have to see it again, to live in my mind through the desecration it suffered and to affirm the major role it now plays in my spiritual life. We approach its golden roofs glittering in the morning sunshine. The sight is stunning, beautiful and humbling. For four hundred and fifty years it has been the seat of our faith and the repository of our learning.

We cross Amritsar – the pool of water surrounding the temple that gave its name to the town. Amritsar – the pool of Nectar of Immortality. We enter the Gurdwara by way of one of its four main gates: one gate on each side to symbolise the openness of our faith to all people, all colours, all creeds. Soon we are lost in wonder at the beauty of the interior, its icons, its artefacts, its great spaces. The temple houses the Adi Granth – the texts and compositions of all of our greatest gurus. We stand before the Akal Takht. It is considered to be the highest seat of justice and authority of the Khalsa and Uncle Gurdip tells us that, of all areas of the temple, it suffered the most at the hands of Ghandi's troops.

"The government attempted to reconstruct it, but we were having none of it," whispers Uncle Gurdip. "The new structure was torn down as non-sacred and men came from all over the Punjab to rebuild it in 1986."

At the end of our tour we visit the kitchens. We are but five of the hundred thousand visitors to the temple each day and each and every one of us is offered a free meal of flat bread and lentil soup.

The following day we bid farewell to the members of Jas' extended family, with many a promise to return and an open-ended invitation for them to visit when we have established our new home in England. It is particularly hard to say goodbye to Uncle Gurdip. He's an old man and the sad fact is that I am unlikely to see him alive again. He has opened my mind to Sikhdom like no one else and I am deeply in his debt.

When the family are safely asleep on the way home, I want to revisit what I have learned. It is as though I fear

77

that flying westward with my back to India, I'll lose my grip on the new parts of me. The jet is equipped with Internet access and my request for a terminal is instantly fulfilled. I find that Uncle Gurdip's estimate of three thousand killed in the Sikh Genocide, was no more than those killed in the capital. No one knows the true total, as the authorities ordered instant cremations to hide the crime from the eyes of international observers. Beyond the capital, in the towns and villages, as many as twenty thousand were thought to have died. A genocide indeed.

I find a speech from 2005 made by Prime Minister Manmohan Singh:

"I have no hesitation in apologising, not only to the Sikh community, but to the whole nation because what took place in 1984 is a negation of the concept of nationhood enshrined in our Constitution. The past is behind us. We cannot change it, but we can write the future. We must have the willpower to write a better future for all of us."

And another from 2009 by the Delhi High Court:

Though we boast of being the world's largest democracy and Delhi being its national capital, the sheer mention of the events of 1984 anti-Sikh riots in general and the role played by Delhi police and the State machinery in particular, makes us hang our heads in shame in the eyes of world polity.

Finally before I close the computer, I wonder what happened to Uncle Gurdip's beloved ancestral village and nearby Nankana Sahib, the birthplace of Guru Nanak, both now deep in Moslem territory. I'm happily surprised to learn that Indian Sikhs have been allowed recently to make pilgrimage to Guru Nanak's birthplace. Furthermore, it is to be awarded Holy City status and the

Government of Pakistan is building a Guru Nanak University in Nankana Sahib. India and Pakistan continue to have an uneasy relationship, but hope springs eternal and Pakistan is welcoming back Sikhs to their holy areas.

I am tired, chastened by what I've learned, and fearful of what lies ahead. I fall asleep hoping that somehow I can bridge the unbridgeable and resolve the irresolvable. I feel I am India personified: seething with contradiction, a blend of hope and aspiration, between the darkness of the past and the aspirations of a better, cleaner future.

5

We've been staying at the Himley House Hotel for three weeks, whilst looking around for our dream house. I did think seriously about moving away from the area altogether, but where to? I know and understand the Black Country. There's every chance I'd feel as out of place in Maidstone or Margate as I did in Majitha. Then there's schools, Jas's many mates, my love of Ma Pardoe's bitter, faggots and peas and Amal's favourite place on earth: Himley Hall. All in all, we've decided to stay local. As they say: a criminal always returns to the scene of his crime.

Jas can't understand why I've insisted upon a low profile. I've told her it's to discourage the begging letters, would-be kidnappers and false friends. She thinks I'm paranoid. If it had been down to her, we'd have done something similar to what Balkar had in mind: gone public and held a big Black Country party for everyone we know. Word *has* got out however and we've entertained a few trusted friends – at our expense, of course.

I've had to go backwards and forwards to the shop. Jas won't go anywhere near it, not even to pack. We've put in a temporary manager and it's on the market, priced for a quick sale. Poor Isha, we let her down badly. She turned up for work the day after we left, to find us gone. I've met with her dad and made it up to her with two months' salary, in lieu. I've kept away from Balkar. Just can't face him. It's the guilt, of course, seeing him would be an overwhelming reminder of the enormity of what I've done.

Finding the right property is a big, big deal. On a daily basis we're turning our noses up at places that were beyond our wildest dreams a little more than a month ago. When I brought Jas to this country, our first home was a sixteenth-floor flat at the top end of Brierley Hill. The views were spectacular but the tower swayed in the wind in winter. We were happy enough at first, together, independent and in love. After Sangi was born, Jas became more and more worried about the lifts and the child having nowhere to play. Maybe her fears brought about a self-fulfilling prophesy: when Sangi was five, she and Jas were trapped in the lift for two hours with a tattooed Hell's Angel chick. Jas and our daughter were OK, but the Hell's Angel had hysterics and peed all over the floor.

Shortly afterwards, we moved to a little terraced house in Lye and Amal was born. It had a postage-stamp sized garden for the children to play in, but we lost the benefit of central-heating. For a girl from the heat of the Punjab, it must have been her worst nightmare. In winter, we wore our outside clothes indoors and huddled against the inadequate electric wall heaters for warmth. Later, with the move to the shop, we regained the benefit of central-heating but lost the garden to a rat-infested shed, four dustbins and an eight by ten concrete storage area.

The house we've finally chosen is near Bobbington, out in the leafy Staffordshire lanes, about five miles from our hotel and ten from Dudley. It's not Black Country proper, but well within spitting distance. The added bonus is that there's a busy little airport out here at Halfpenny Green and Amal will be able to indulge his latest obsession for planes. We still have to pinch ourselves every time we look at the property details: six bedrooms, indoor swimming pool and gym, large games room, library, Sangi's very own music room, breakfast kitchen (the size of a Sikh temple), magnificent wood-panelled lounge overlooking three and a half acres of grounds. Needless to say, there's also a huge double garage, a workshop, green housing, a formal garden, a large vegetable patch, a small orchard and a large sweeping drive down to automatic double gates. We've haggled over the price – an exercise that both the elderly owner and our 'posh-end' estate agent seemed to regard as rather vulgar. Vulgar or not, the gent came down by two hundred thousand to a cool one and three quarter million. We're well-pleased as it's the first time we've economised in any way since 'winning' the money. The two hundred grand will more than cover our chosen cars, even with our top-spec customised preferences: Jas wants a red Audi A5 Cabriolet and I've put myself down for an all-new silver Range Rover Sport.

Both kids get to stay at their present schools – which has always been part of the plan. Once we're settled, there'll be specialised extra home-tuition for Amal and Sangi will be able to travel up to Birmingham on Saturdays to get her additional violin classes. Sangi's over the moon and talking already about getting a pony. It's not such a bad idea as Amal could learn to ride too and animals are regarded as effective autistic therapy. We'll probably have to add a stable to the property's already ample amenities.

Since India, I've been living in a kind of purposeful daze. The trip continues to have a deep effect upon me and I've still no idea of how I'm going to reconcile my deeper understanding of Sikhism with the abiding guilt. I know what Christians mean when they say, 'I've sold my soul to the Devil'. I've brought such transparent, effervescent happiness to the family – but will it ever make it right? For now, I'm trying to pack enough activity into the space of each day to keep the personal demons at bay. It's worked so far, but what happens when life settles to the snail pace of an idle country squire?

Yesterday morning we signed the contracts and were given next Tuesday as our moving-in date. It's been one long giddy round of anticipatory spending – traipsing the best stores of Birmingham, Wolverhampton and Merry Hill with a mission to equip the new property with furniture, bedding, kitchen and media equipment. Bored sales staff turn into attentive sycophants as soon as they catch wind of our spending power. It's a too frequent response that reluctantly I'm having to get used to.

We're in at last! Jas and I take a tour of the garden and the kids follow. Is this how the Ward family, the former Lords of Dudley felt when they strutted their stuff around Himley Hall? I've never seen Amal so agitated. He knows for sure that this is his new home. Every two yards or so, he stops to examine a plant, a flower, a clump of grass. He pulls his sister this way and that, and despite her good nature I can see her frustration rising. Poor Sangita, but for now she'll have to cope; this is *our* moment – mine and Jas's. I've brought (or maybe bought?) her happiness at last. Later, when the children are fast asleep on temporary mattresses in their vast new bedrooms, I pull her down beside me and slowly, leisurely, we begin to make love. Soon I'm stifling her moans, lest the children hear and take fright that banshees are stalking the corridors.

It's a whole new world out here. We're awakened by birdsong and the crowing of a distant rooster. We're no longer surrounded by mean streets and litter and drunken carousers, they've been replaced by gardens and fields and trees swaying in the early summer breeze. Our nearest neighbour is Mrs Ashton, a goat farmer. She comes over on the first morning to welcome us. She sells the milk to hospitals as far away as Shrewsbury – apparently it's good for a whole range of allergic conditions. She spins the wool herself too and makes the finest Angora sweaters. She takes to Amal immediately and tells us that her sister's boy has a similar condition. Before long he's on his way with her to see the goats and we're told not to worry, he'll be back in an hour or two.

Busy, exhausting days follow: pushing and pulling furniture around, arranging things as we want, receiving deliveries, directing plasterers, plumbers, electricians, carpenters, painters and decorators, hopping from room to room with teas and coffees to keep happy the magicians who are transforming a house to a home. We splash around in the indoor pool each night; it's our reward for the day's labour. We leap and shout and duck each other, washing out the fatigue and revelling in the intimate joy of family. The new stable is erected, we go visiting horsey folk with their fruity country accents and their jodhpurs and hacking jackets.

The pony is chosen and the lady at the stables takes a shine to Sangita. She promises to advise on clothes and tack and offers the children free riding lessons. Jas's eyes are shining; I think she's made another friend and the riding school is less than a mile from our new estate. We return home in the comfortable luxury of my silver Range Rover Sport. Jas and Sangi are singing a pop song and Amal is rocking back and forth to their efforts, his back slapping rhythmically against the soft leather of the seat. Happy Families – the new name of the game. We're home and our impressive garden gates swing back majestically to allow us in. Jas's sleek Audi Quattro graces the front of the house, crouching there, waiting like a hunting tiger. My wife throws me a Blackpool Illuminations smile and goes off with the kids to pick raspberries for supper.

I sit watching them from the lounge. I've treated myself to a small whisky, a Glen Moray. I know that Jas is unhappy that the whisky didn't end with what she sees as our escape from drudgery and debt. She says nothing and I know I'm trading on her gratitude. She's a woman transformed. The tired, careworn individual who snapped at customers and cried herself to sleep has gone and not even a shadow remains. Even in this short time, she's joined a golf club and taken out membership of a health club and spa. I've pointed out jokingly that we've got virtual golf in the games room and our gym's probably better equipped than the health club. I know that's not the point; Jas is a social animal, she needs company – not the 'riff-raff' of Netherton, as she called them – but successful, interesting, well-heeled, ladies of leisure, with no axes to grind.

The family enters through the large French windows carrying a pile of fresh-picked fruit. Jas is flushed and giggling like a young girl. She crosses to me and I get a peck on the cheek.

"I've been thinking, Rakki," she says. "I want to call the place, 'Harnoor', because it's God's Gift."

I beam my approval and feel my chest tighten unbearably. There could be no bigger blasphemy, no greater irony. A wave of misery crashes over me as she bends and lightly kisses me again before heading off to the kitchen. I reach for the bottle, pour myself a much larger shot and stand gazing out over the lawns. How in hell am I going to carry on living with myself?

6

It's been six weeks. The school holidays are approaching but we've decided to stay put. Being here is like one long holiday anyway. I've had a tennis court built and we've fenced off part of the garden as a paddock for Ginger, the new pony. Sangi loves him with a passion and spends hours grooming him, talking to him and riding him around the paddock. Amal is less keen than we expected. It was a disappointment; a lot of autistic kids take very well to horses and sometimes show them more emotion than they show their families. He'll ride when Sangi leads Ginger around by the reins, but there's no real bonding. He'd rather go and play with the goats next door.

His school will be running a morning holiday club, so there'll be some relief for us. It does mean that Jas and I will have to continue to take it in turn on the school run. The school bus doesn't come out this far. The afternoons will be covered by a local girl called Sarah Jennings. She's a nice kid, in her second year at university, so she jumped at the chance of some regular vacation earnings. He's much calmer these days and almost completely off medication – more generally responsive than ever he was at the shop. There's been another new development: the school staff became very excited when he began learning chess. They were astonished at the speed in which he progressed through the levels. I was called in at the point when he reached Level Ten and was frequently beating the machine. As with anything else that really grabs him, for a time it's pretty much to the exclusion of all else. According to Mr Price, his teacher, he's reached the equivalent of Junior Grand Master level within six months.

It's clear that Amal has some pretty extraordinary abilities. It's as if all of his mental energy becomes focussed on one singular mental effort. It's not an uncommon characteristic in people like him and was highlighted in the film *Rain Man,* when Dustin Hoffman played the autistic character, Raymond. Raymond could count all of the cards in a six-deck shoe and won a fortune for his brother in a Las Vegas casino. There's a boy at Amal's school who can tell you what day of the week it was for pretty much any day on the calendar going back fifty years or so. Mr Price asked if he could begin to enter Amal for live chess competitions, but Jas and I have refused. We don't want Amal paraded as some freak of nature who can do extraordinary mental tricks. *Idiot Savants* they were called, historically. I'll kill the first person who calls my Amal *idiot* anything.

We're now into the holidays. Sangita's always been popular at school, but when her mates discovered that her new house sports a swimming pool, a gym, a tennis court and a games room and that there's a pony to ride for good measure, they were soon flocking here in ever increasing numbers. Within two weeks it was beginning to take on the appearance of the Dudley Teenage Holiday Complex, so we've had to lay down a limit of four friends per day. Even so, that's seven kids per afternoon, counting Amal and Sarah, his helper.

Jas and I soon pick up that a lad called Tony Pickles almost always features in the group. His dad is the assistant manager of Lloyds Bank in Dudley. I have an account there, so Dad must be well aware of our change in fortune. When Jas asks Sangi whether she is a little sweet on him, her furious denial confirms our suspicions. I say 'suspicions' because for me in particular, it comes as a bit of a shock. Despite the physical evidence of her growing maturity, for me she's still my little girl. Jas says that's a 'Dad thing' and in time, I'll accept that she's a young woman. I know that this is jumping the gun, but it has to be said too, that it's never occurred to me that any kid of mine might marry outside our Sikh community. When I grew up, I just took it for granted that in spite of being fully assimilated into my school and community, eventually I'd settle down with a Sikh girl. It didn't seem to be particularly racist, it was just what you did.

So, *am* I racist? Shit, maybe I am. Would it be such a terrible thing if Sangi ended up marrying a nice white guy like him? I don't know, the jury's still out. Deep down, like many from my generation of Sikhs, I know I've been guilty of double standards: in my wilder, younger days, I messed about with the odd white girl – because they were the ones that were free, easy and willing. But ask any Sikh what he would do if anyone touched his daughter. That's a different ball game! One of my mates is a Black Country solicitor, he was born at Russell's Hall Hospital, in the same maternity ward as me. He's well educated, cultured and as fully assimilated into western society as I am – or so one would think! When his eighteen-year-old daughter became pregnant by a young Sikh, my friend withdrew twelve grand and put out a contract on the lad's life! In spite of him being a lawyer and fully aware of the potential personal and professional consequences, nothing could dissuade him. The threat was lifted only when the terrified pair agreed to marry and were settled into a loveless partnership. No Siree, you don't mess with a Sikh's daughter. And yes – I've made a mental note to keep a close eye on the handsome Tony Pickles.

Jas is out and about most of the time. Today, she's been at the NEC visiting the Camping and Caravan Show with a couple of new mates, who by the look of them, would never be seen dead in a camp site. She's got it into her head that we need a motor caravan to tour Europe – maybe even the world – and I fear that she might come back with one. All the more the surprise when she returns and parks a mini-bus outside the house.

"I thought it was a motor caravan you were after?" I say with a grin.

"I haven't *bought* it, Silly! I'm driving Samantha Godson for a bridal fitting tomorrow. You know, the girl from the estate agency who found us the house? Then we're off to her hen party in Birmingham, with a bunch of her friends. She's hired it for me."

"Useful thing, a teetotal mate, when it comes to driving back from parties."

She takes it the wrong way. "She really likes me. I'd have been invited anyway."

"I didn't mean it like that."

"Anyway, I'm off to bed. Big day ahead. What are your plans?"

"I'm golfing in the morning. Arnold seems to think I'm ready for a proper game."

"Oh that's good! I knew you'd get there in the end." She's a much better golfer than me and trying hard to keep any hint of condescension from her voice.

"We'll see, we'll see. I'll be up to bed soon."

Her face falls. "Don't get drinking too much, will you, Rakki?"

I'm irritated by the remark – unjustly so, because she's guessed I'm going to take a little nip or two. Am I really so transparent? Can't a guy just have a quiet nightcap?

"I *never* drink too much."

"Anyway, Sarah can't make it tomorrow afternoon and Sangi's out, so can you be sure to make it back by two, to take over with Amal?"

"No problem."

"Goodnight, then."

I go over to the drinks cabinet and fetch a bottle and glass, then make a trip to the kitchen and hold the glass under the ice dispenser. Back in the lounge I pour myself a generous measure. Snap, crackle, pop. Ah, the old amber nectar. It's the only sensible response. Better by far than falling apart. It keeps me strong, allows me to function. I've more than enough to feel guilty about, without adding a weakness for the odd whisky.

Jas is so *grounded* these days, happy, fulfilled – whole. I wish I could say the same about me. Her golf has really taken off. As I told Sangi – her Mum was good, even back in the old Himley public course days. According to her coach, she has the makings of a top player. Maybe it's something they tell all of their wealthy clients, to keep the tuition fees flowing? On the other hand, that's certainly not what my coach has been telling me! He goes around looking as glum as a car-sick driving instructor and I see genuine pain in his eyes when I slice ball after ball into the rough, or hack out yet another huge divot from the fairway. I'm a huge disappointment to him: I'm a bloody huge disappointment to myself. Subconsciously, I suppose I believed that I'd streak ahead of Jas as I was quite a sportsman in my youth. As for her, before she met me, sport was just something sweaty and nasty that was undertaken by consenting males.

Her second new passion is spa visits, she insists they're essential for her health and beauty. I'd be the last to argue against it, as she's been looking more and more stunning as the weeks pass. She tells me about skin treatments, muscle treatments, facials, all-over body therapy, hair treatments, eye treatments, nail treatments; the list is endless and I pretend interest. If I'm honest, all that matters to me is that she comes home each day with a smile on her face. Her circle of friends has increased dramatically. She's picked up again with some from before, but others saddened her with their ill-concealed jealousy. There's been no shortage of replacements – attractive, well-groomed, well-heeled girls with all of the time in the world on their hands. There seems to be some kind of inverse ratio afoot – I've had the misfortune of meeting one or two of their husbands, pale exhausted types, absorbed in making the fortunes that their wives so willingly spend.

I feel lonely, isolated, lost and bored without the shop and my colourful customers. I take another measure of the malt and assure myself that the booze is well under control. The guilt sits less heavily upon my shoulders when I take a dram, but I can't deny that there's a gathering cloud of negativity about me. I know that Jas and I never felt the same way about the shop. I loved it, especially the sharing of ordinary people's lives and problems. That's what Sikhism is really all about:

community and belonging. Sikhism is expressed through our meaningful dealings with others. Bloody great! Just what meaningful dealings with others am I having these days? Inside, I feel I'm just an ordinary working bloke, an ex-postman, son of a foundry worker. I dreamed of money, of course, but it was money to stem the tide of debt, to cut away from the stress of constantly picking up yet another bill from a supplier or the tax man and now that's all passed. Life is easy, comfortable and stress free, but it's empty too, frivolous and shallow.

I refill the glass with ice, pour the malt through it and listen to the satisfying crackle.

I've tried to talk through these feelings with Jas – not the crime behind them, of course – but it's beyond her understanding that I can be yearning for the life we left behind. Worse still, it makes her insecure, threatens her new sense of well-being. At times she sympathises. 'But go back to the Gurdwara, Rakki,' she'll say. 'Go and socialise there. You'll rediscover that sense of meaning. Find a charity that you can identify with. Give some time to it, it's one of our sacred duties.' At other times, she's angry and indignant. 'Cheer up, for God's sake! What's so difficult? What have *you* given up, by comparison with me? Don't you think I gave up *everything* when I came here: my family, a chance of a career, my friends, my society – all for you and this cold, rain-swept land?' At times like that she thinks I'm rocking the boat, tempting Fate, spitting in the face of Lady Fortune – and then we begin one of our more serious fallings-out.

Would she have stayed happy if we'd never gone near the shop and I'd have remained a postman and her an office secretary? I think that she probably would. When I brought her over, she thought that the streets of England were paved with gold. At first, even the wind-swept tower block was a palace to a girl from Majitha. Her secretarial job gave her status too. But then came the shop. It was the making of me and it dragged her down. She was too fierce, too proud, too straight, too educated maybe, to deal with the eccentric, the embittered, the mean and the alcoholic. Out here, she's found her feet again, in the bosom of privilege; mixing with the types who have the time and the money to be relaxed, amusing and generous in their friendships. And so we live the life of comfortable frivolity. I continue to try to fit in, hoping that the black cloud will disperse, drinking more than I know I should, hoping that through the new happiness of my family, the day will come when I can live with myself and eventually even come to forgive myself.

I tiptoe to bed. Jas is asleep already. The bed's such a huge fucking size that there's no danger of waking her.

I'm nervous on the way to the game. Stupid! The whole point of playing is to *enjoy*. Relax and enjoy! Arnold has found me three regular members who are short of a fourth man. We're set for eighteen holes. The problem is I know for sure now that I'm not a golfing natural. In spite of my past sporting credentials, out on the course I feel ungainly and poorly coordinated. Oh *fuck it!* It's not World War Three, it's just a bunch of guys with sticks and balls! I've spent hours on the driving range whacking away with the woods, I've putted until my brain is putty and learned all the theory there is to know about the purpose of the various irons. I'm going to be fine.

They seem patient enough at the beginning and give me the, 'Don't worry, old man, we all have to start somewhere,' routine. By the third hole, I'm making a total arse of myself. The more I hack the rough to pieces, the more I take six or seven swipes off the tees, the more time I spend hopelessly hunting lost balls, the more their mood changes. On some holes I just pick up the ball rather than keep them waiting any longer. At last, it's over. As we make our way over to the clubhouse, they're muttering amongst themselves and barely speaking to me. Ignorant bastards. They needed a make-weight and they were fully aware that I was a rank amateur.

We retire to the bar. At least that's one place where I come second to no man. I hasten over to Dean, the barman, anxious to get in the first round to ensure that I can double up on my own whisky.

Jim Brennan, a retired dentist, attempts to recover some of his earlier civility. "Don't worry about the game too much, old man," he says. "Practice makes perfect, you need more time with the coach, more time on the driving range."

I shrug and put my hands palms upward. I'm not giving them the satisfaction of an apology. They're a civilised bunch and now it's all over, they do their best to twist their faces into expressions of bonhomie. I feel patronised and take a long pull at my over-sized whisky. I'm rapidly coming to the conclusion that I don't particularly like the game anyway. These guys are self-made men and so self-assured. They have no idea that I'm a bloody imposter, standing in for a bloke who's probably sitting on the pavement in Netherton right now, pissed out of his skull. The whisky's not working its usual magic. I'm feeling more and more pissed off. It's a game for toffs – what the hell am I *doing* in here? I'm overtaken by a sudden self-hatred. I recognise a 'little man' inside who doesn't feel comfortable in posh circles. A man who never feels quite good enough. Is it the legacy of growing up motherless, poor and working class in a Black Country back street? Or is it something more sinister? A throwback to the Indian native, in the shadow of his colonial masters? I fucking hope not.

"Jim's right about the additional practice: very wise," Malcolm Redwood is saying.

I feel like awarding him a prize for today's statement of the totally bleeding obvious. He's dressed in full plus fours and looks as though he was *born* on a green. He plays off a five handicap and must have found my performance excruciating.

"I'll get back to Arnold," I reply. "Book some more coaching sessions. Looking on the bright side, I can only get better."

There's general embarrassment.

"Must have a word with Arnold," says Malcolm, absently.

Tim Merryman, the fourth member of our group returns with more drinks. I realise with a start that if I don't get a move on, I'm going to be late back for Jas and her driving mission. I down the new double and offer my apologies for a hasty departure. They can hardly mask their relief and I know that, even if by some remote chance I wanted to, I'm not going to be playing with them any time soon. I stride out and fling my gleaming new clubs into the back of the Range Rover with a savagery that turns the heads of a couple of passing members. It takes just seconds to tear my scorecard into a handful of confetti and allow the breeze to distribute it across the car park.

I drive home at lunatic speed, but Jas is waiting already by the side of the minibus and she's not looking best pleased.

"We said two o'clock," she says by way of greeting.

"It's only ten past! Sorry, the game took longer than expected."

"The nineteenth hole, you mean? You stink of booze."

"I don't *stink* of booze! I had a very quick one with them. You can't just walk away, you know that."

She wants to make amends. "Anyway, you enjoyed it?"

"Yeah, great. First time out in a proper game."

"I'm pleased and you think you're going to like it?"

I try to look enthusiastic. "Not sure it grabs me in quite the way it grabs you, but yeah, it's OK."

She pulls a wry face. There's no way of reading it: disappointment that I'm not an enthusiast, concern about my drinking, annoyance with my tetchiness, fear that I'm no nearer towards settling down, or just pure anxiety over being late? Whatever. She's not a happy bunny.

"I've got to run," she says. "I've left you a tuna salad, if you're hungry. Tell Liz to go back to the cleaning now. I asked her to keep an eye on Amal until you got back."

"OK, Love. Have fun."

She takes off like a Formula One driver, scattering gravel out into both sides of the lawn. I make a tour of the gardens to cool off before taking over responsibility for my son. The grounds are looking slightly the worse for wear. We've put money into the paddock and the tennis court but neglected general maintenance. The allotment is weedy, the lawns are a little overgrown and the flower beds are straggly and untidy. The old chap who sold us the place used to do everything himself, so Jas and I got to thinking that it would be well within our capabilities. I found out quickly that I don't have green fingers – nor the enthusiasm, to be fair – and Jas, well Jas doesn't get her hands dirty these days. Jas is jazzing about too much in her new whirlwind life. I like the pun: *Jas jazzing about.*

After a quick bite, I lead Amal out to the sit-on mower. He jumps up on my lap and off we go. We've done the lawns this way once before and he loves it. It's easy work, I just sit and steer and empty the grass box from time to time. Backwards and forwards, up and down, it's very relaxing and I take pleasure in making perfect stripes. I guess long-term, I'll have to get us a gardener, at least a part-time one. It would be a crime to let these beautiful grounds go to rack and ruin and with very little effort, we could easily grow some fruit and vegetables.

Jas gets back at nine, taking me by surprise. Amal's asleep already and Sangita's taking a late dip in the pool. I'm sprawled in front of our wall-to-wall telly in the lounge and there's a half bottle of whisky in front of me and an ice tray. Jas takes in the booze with a look of intense disapproval.

"I dropped everyone off except Samantha," she says, "and what a mistake that turned out to be!"

"Oh, how's that?"

"I had to take back the minibus and pick up my car. Samantha was semi-conscious on the back seat; they'd been mixing her drinks all evening. Anyway the bloke at the car hire helped me to transfer her to my car, then on the way to her place, she was sick all over everywhere."

"Great! Why do they get pissed like that? So un-ladylike."

"Well, *you're* one to talk!"

I'm instantly angry. "Come on, Jas! What a bloody thing to say!"

"I count the empties, Rakesh. Do you have any idea of what you're getting through?"

"It's just a temporary thing. Adjustment. I can stop any time I like."

"Well, bloody stop then!" she snaps. The vehemence shocks me. "Do you see *me* drinking? You're a Sikh for God's sake, it's a sin! What kind of example do you think you give to Sangita?"

That one hurts and I've no defence. "Didn't think you felt *that* strongly," I say, lamely. "Anyway, she's fine. She's taking a swim."

"Fine, *fine*. Everything's fine. "Has it even come to your notice that her music's dropped off?"

That one takes me by surprise, but I'm glad of the shift in focus. "Dropped off?"

"Stopped, ceased, desisted!"

"You're serious?"

She sighs heavily and climbs down a little. "Maybe that's putting it too strongly. She's still doing her practice, but she's less keen that's for sure. Maybe it's just her age, the hormones, her need for a little freedom. I hope it's nothing to do with moving here."

"You're losing me more and more, Jas."

The impatience returns. "She's running around with that bunch of kids that come here. That's where she's been tonight. Haven't you even asked her?"

I'm alarmed now. "Been – where?"

"Just hanging out at each other's houses I suppose. Like they do when they come here."

"Well, there's not a lot wrong with that – if that's all it is. They're a nice enough crowd, aren't they?"

"They are, and I'm not suggesting that she's doing anything wrong or has anything to hide. There's one exception – she confessed today that she's missed her last three Saturday practice sessions in Birmingham."

"Why?"

"She's been meeting up with her mates over there instead."

"And that Tony Pickles is amongst them?"

"More than likely. She talks about him all the time."

My face must have given away more than I intended.

"That's no problem, is it – a non-Sikh boy?" she asks.

"Well, I'm hoping it's a bit bloody premature to be talking like that."

"I know. But, you know what I mean."

"At the moment, I'm more worried about what you've said about her music. She's wanted nothing else but the RCM for the past three years."

"It wouldn't worry me you know, a non-Sikh boy. Times are changing, I know of at least two mixed marriages in local Sikh families."

"Jas, can we drop that! I'll have to have a word with her about her music though."

"Well, make sure you do it in a roundabout way. Ask her how it's progressing. I've broken my word, in telling you about Saturdays."

This is a new departure, Jas and Sangi having secrets from me. Or is it? I'm tired, she's tired, there's no point in pursuing it further tonight.

"Let's call it a day now, shall we? I did the lawns with Amal this afternoon, I'm knackered."

"Promise me you'll do something about the drinking."

"*It's not a big deal.* I keep telling you."

"OK, OK. Don't start getting excited about it."

I get myself back under control. "Tell you what, I'll clean up your car for you in the morning."

She looks pleased. She'll be wanting to get to her yoga class for eleven and I feel a twinge of guilt because I know exactly what I'm doing – I'm softening her up for the bedroom. Things have gone a little off the boil in that department, lately.

Sangi comes through from the pool and wishes us goodnight. We go up and Jas takes a quick shower to get rid of the smell of Samantha. I'm in bed already, lying waiting with an anticipatory erection. She's perfumed and wearing a shortie nightie, looking every inch as desirable as on our honeymoon night. She faces towards me and kisses me on the forehead.

"You are going to be happy here, aren't you?" she asks.

"Of course I am," I reassure her. "Who wouldn't be? It's a dream come true."

I pull her towards me and she immediately begins to respond.

I feel myself shrink. It's the first time it's happened since Amritsar.

7

I've opened a new shop. I'm hoping that it will be provide the antidote I need: back in harness, feeling useful, making a difference, being part of the community again. I made a successful bid for a large modern unit in Norton on the edge of Stourbridge: there was a niche there, a need for a decent supermarket and Norton is a busy, upmarket suburb far enough from the town not to be affected by the Tescos and Sainsburys of this world. We've just completed our first fortnight's trading and I've been going in every day. There'll be no going back to the bad old days of six and a half days a week – I'm daft, but I'm not stupid! I've appointed a young guy called Geoff Richards to manage the place and to my great joy, when our old assistant, Isha, heard about my plans she resigned her job and came back to work for me.

From next week I'm planning to cut back to doing just half days. Geoff's making a very good fist of the accounts and stock control and it's clear the place will be in safe hands. Today, I completed the staffing with the addition of two further full-time assistants: an Indian lad called Dev, fresh from school and Jim Knight, a bloke of near-pension age who was recommended by a friend.

At first, Jas thought I was insane, but it was money that finally won the argument. At the old shop, she'd never face up to our financial situation, she was just mega-miserable about the spending cuts I imposed. Now our fortunes have reversed and although she'd still rather leave budgets and investments to me and simply enjoy the spending, finally, I've managed to make her sit down and listen.

I've explained: we may be wealthy now, but everything's relative: if you don't capitalise upon your wealth it will deteriorate. Four point six million *is* a hell of a lot of money, but then we've begun to *spend:* we paid off the old shop at a loss and settled with the remainder of our debtors, we set up Jas's relatives in India, we spent close on two million upon our house and cars. We didn't stop there, of course: there's been all of the 'must have' home additions and improvements. All in all, about two million quid remained for rock solid investment and around a hundred thousand in liquidity.

Camelot's financial gurus taught me about ultra-safe investments with a regular permanent return on capital. There's a Risk Factor Index: the band I opted for was for shares and funds predicting between a low of two and a half per cent and a high of five per cent annual return upon capital. The problem with conservative investment is, of course, that it produces conservative returns. Without any specialised knowledge you can work out a best and worst case scenario on the back of a fag packet: best case, two million gives you a five per cent annual return: one hundred grand; worst case (a bad year on the financial markets), it returns two and a half per cent: fifty grand.

Even Jas could see the red light on that one: worst case, we'd collect fifty grand; which is not a whole lot more than a couple of married teachers can expect, in the early years of their career. It's undeniable that only months ago, fifty grand a year was an impossible dream. Now, it looks like small beer when set against our outgoings: a massive rates bill, a power bill that includes keeping an indoor swimming pool at the blood warm temperature preferred by Jas; a stable, a part-time cook/cleaner, etc. etc. Plus all of the jollies, clubs and societies that keep Jas healthy and happy and the additional tuition and help that we've brought in for Amal. Add to that the money we send to India and suddenly, we don't seem that rich any more.

Those were the arguments that I used to help Jas see that gaining a substantial secondary income from a profitable supermarket was not such a bad idea. Of course, in her financial education, I tended to stress the worst case scenario, but that was justifiable gamesmanship. I wanted the supermarket so badly. She's seen the change in me, too; I feel energised, I'm drinking less and I'm probably a nicer bloke to know.

Another two weeks of intensive commercial activity have passed and I've just completed a review of the first month of trading. I should be pleased: turnover has been thirty per cent above my best opening estimate. At that rate, it suggests an end-of-year profit of around one hundred thousand pounds. Jas is delighted with the news. I've stopped talking about a slow capital leakage scenario and she can see that she's in a position to maintain her high spending life style.

I say I should be pleased. The reason I'm *not* pleased is totally perverse: it's just that the team has gelled around Geoff Richards. He's not just a good manager, he's bloody *brilliant*. He's so good that when I go in to oversee things, I'm beginning to feel more and more like a spare dinner.

I'm no hypocrite, I'm delighted with the additional family income, but of course, it was never my main motivation. I wanted to remain really hands on – the vital mainspring of the organisation, the life and soul of its commercial success, on first name terms with the majority of my customers. I saw it as my rebirth and at first, that's the way it was. Grudgingly, I've had to accept that if I'm not there all of the time, the mantle will pass to Geoff. Since he's found his feet, whatever I suggest has been thought through already, or is about to be done, or already *has* been done. The shop hums with his vitality, his rigour, his attention to detail, his charisma and his excellent relationships with customers and staff. All of that is *chink, chink,* in my pocket and meanwhile, I'm back to wondering what the fuck I'm going to do with my life.

Jas must have noticed the change in me and she challenges me at dinner. "Have you gone a bit cool on the shop lately?"

I'm instantly prickly and defensive. "Whatever gave you that idea? I've told you how well we've been doing."

"You don't seem that pleased, lately."

"I'm pleased; for God's sake, I'm *pleased.*"

I've raised my voice and I'm close to shouting. Sangi and her mother look one to the other. I'm in the doghouse and Jas picks up the baton.

"You know, I just can't think what's got into you, Rakki? God smiles upon us with the Lottery good fortune and before long, you're as miserable as sin. You open a new shop and it's all smiles again, then before I can turn around, you're acting as though the sky's fallen in!"

"That's *rubbish!* I'm perfectly OK; it's not you that has to do all of the worrying, that's all!"

"What worrying? What *is* there to worry about? Tell me! We've been blessed with everything we could ever wish for, yet ever since the win, you've been a changed man."

"And you? Don't you think you're a changed woman?"

That angers her. "At least I'm out there enjoying myself! Thanking God every day for my good fortune and trying to make the best of it! And don't tell me your drinking's under control! Changing to vodka hasn't fooled me. I don't need to *smell* it, you know!"

Our argument is arrested by a massive crashing sound. We both turn and see that Sangita has thrown her dinner plate to the floor and is running tearfully from the room. Even Amal raises his head and stops his rocking.

"Now look what you've done!" shouts Jas.

I rise from my chair and follow Sangi upstairs. Her bedroom door is shut but I knock and walk on in. She's lying across her bed, sobbing pitifully.

"Sangi, Sangi," I say and begin gently to stroke her beautiful, dark hair.

"Does it mean that you and Mummy are going to divorce?" she gasps between her sobs.

"Oh Sangi," Her words upset me to the core. "Whatever would make you think that?"

"Because you're always so *unhappy* since we moved and Mum is always talking about it. And you're living separate lives."

"I'm not unhappy! We don't lead separate lives."

"You *are,* you *are!* Before, you were always laughing and joking, even when you were tired, even when we had no money."

"It's difficult. I don't want to tell you lies. I don't find it easy, all this money, this new way of life."

"Why? *We're* all happy, why can't you be?"

"I don't know. I can't tell you the cause. I'm sure it's going to get better."

"And you're not unhappy with Mummy?"

"Of course I'm not unhappy with Mummy, Sweetheart! Your mummy's my life! And anyway, how many divorced Sikhs have you ever met?"

"But you never see each other. She goes out to do her things, you go out to the shop or just seem to sit around here."

"Yes, but we're -"

"Tony's mum and dad are getting divorced. He's so unhappy, it frightens me."

"Who's Tone – Ah! Your friend, the blonde boy?" She nods and I see that she's drying her tears. "That's very sad. He's a really good friend, isn't he?"

"I think I love him, Daddy. Is that OK? He's the nicest boy in the world."

I swallow hard and struggle to keep my expression neutral. "Well, I expect you'll love lots of people before you're really ready to settle down?"

She shakes her head determinedly. "No, he's going to do physics and I'm going to do music and then when we've finished at university, he's going to ask you if he can marry me."

"Well, a lot can happen before then. You might even meet a nice Sikh boy."

"It doesn't have to be a Sikh boy, does it, Daddy? I've asked Mum."

"Well, I'd always thought -"

"You've always said that everyone's as good as everyone else."

She has me over a Sikh barrel now. "Well, yes, that's very true."

"Anyway, I've been thinking of not doing music. Like that, we could both be at the same university."

That *is* one step too far.

"Oh well, I *would* put my foot down at that, Sangi. Let's just try to take things one step at a time, shall we? I hope that you're keeping up your practice, attending on Saturdays and trying as hard as ever?" Her look tells me everything. "If ever your mum and I were expected to give our blessing to a man that you chose from the outside, we'd have to be very sure that you'd tested the relationship against time and had followed your own career path first."

"And then you might say yes?"

Her eyes have grown even bigger and rounder than normal.

"And then, I suppose we'd have to see."

Sangi puts her arms around me. "Oh I do love you, Daddy."

"And I love you too, Darling. Now, dry your tears and no more worrying about Mum and me. We're just busy trying to find our own new paths through it all. And don't you dare ever let up on that violin!"

8

Arnold rings me on Monday morning to say he's found me a partner for a game this afternoon.

"He's a very pleasant bloke. A new member – more your level," he tells me.

"Totally crap, then?"

He laughs down the phone. "Don't take it like that, Rakesh, we all have to start somewhere."

"I've heard that somewhere before! No more Jims, Tims and Malcolms, for a while then? Did Malcolm 'have a word', as he put it?"

He sounds embarrassed. "He mentioned that you struggled and that the game was somewhat slow. My fault – I paired you with them because I felt that you were all compatible."

"All really well-heeled, you mean?"

"Well, since you put it like that – yes."

"I was kinda hoping that flash clubs and clothes would have turned me into Tiger Woods by now."

"See how you get on with this Dave Taylor. He's an engineer and he's been playing a month less than you. I've booked you in for two o'clock. You both have a similar style."

I put down the phone and laugh out loud. 'You both have a similar style.' Good old Arnold. I picture Dave Taylor missing his ball a dozen times on the first tee, slashing away until he's made an open cast mine of the fairway, breaking his clubs over his knee in frustration. Dave Taylor and I have a similar style!

Jas is out all day. She's playing in a minor tournament this morning. She'll either progress to the afternoon quarter final, or stay on to watch the winners. I text her to let her know I'll be out on the fairway in the afternoon and probably back later than her.

I make myself an early lunch: some cold tikka chicken and a couple of chapattis. It deserves a glass of white wine. I open an ice cold Chablis. One glass doesn't seem enough and before I know it, I've finished off the bottle. At least it's steadied the nerves. Stupid to get worked up about the game. I have to keep reminding myself: I play for *pleasure*. I open a second bottle. It's not like whisky – more like drinking water. There's about half an hour before I need to drive over to the club. I go through to the lounge with the bottle, a glass and some cheese biscuits: time to catch up on the news on the wide-screen TV.

Shit – it's twenty to two! The second bottle's empty. I must have dozed off and there's only twenty minutes before I'm due to meet this guy. Wow! I'm really unsteady on my feet. And there was I telling myself that wine had no clout. I shouldn't be driving really. God! I scuff the kerb on a bend and it throws the car into the centre of the road. Lucky nothing was coming the other way. Slow down! But I can't, I'm fucking late now. Finally, I screech to a halt in the members' car park and the dust cloud I've created whirls towards the clubhouse. I half-walk, half-run towards the building. My accelerated heartbeat concentrates the alcohol wonderfully, it firestorms my few remaining brain cells and suddenly, I'm all over the place.

It takes me two attempts to target Dean. First go, I end up at the wrong end of the bar.

"Has anyone been asking after me?" I slur.

I needn't have worried. Dean knows Dave Taylor and says he's not been in yet.

I'm just about to ask him for a strong coffee when I notice there's something going on at the far end of the room. I wander over and someone shoves a glass in my hand. It's a birthday celebration for an elderly geezer I think I recognise.

"Gerry's ninety today," I'm told. "He's our oldest member!"

Good old Gerry! I hold out the glass and somebody fills it with champagne. I offer Gerry a toast. The old fella gets hold of a bottle and promptly fills my glass again. Good old Gerry! And this stuff is so much better than the lunchtime Chablis. I drink it down – must get some in for my cellar. Gerry's now my very best friend, he's topping me up again.

A hand taps my shoulder. "Is it Rakesh?"

I stare through the fog at a middle-aged bloke who seems to be demanding something of me.

"I'm Dave," he says.

"Dave who?"

"Dave Taylor. I think we're booked down for a game together?"

"Is it today?" I ask.

He gives me a funny look. I follow him down to the changing rooms and somehow I find the right key to my locker. I stand there like an idiot, staring at the empty inside.

"Fuck, it's empty," I inform him.

"Are you sure you're all right to play?"

"Got it!" I tell him. "My stuff's in the car."

"Look, Rakesh, we can play another time?"

I won't hear of it. I ask him to hold on a minute or two whilst I return to the car.

Fresh air! But it doesn't seem to be helping me to open the car. Good! Finally – and there's the bloody golf bag, in the boot!

Blackness.

The ultimate humiliation, Jas has come to collect me. They telephoned her from the club. I'm in a large armchair in the member's lounge. I've no idea how I got there. I can't believe it's more than four hours since I walked into the club. Jas tells me in a voice that fills me with foreboding that I was *dragged* there – after being found semi-conscious by the side of my car.

We leave in her car, of course, and Jas is barely speaking to me. Aw, fuck it! It's not the end of the world. So I had a few drinks. I try telling her that it was the champagne, not a drink I'm used to. Big mistake! She wants to know what champagne's got to do with empty Chablis bottles, in the lounge, back home.

It takes four days and some heavy promises before I'm back in favour. It's Friday and we have a free week-end ahead of us: 'free' in the sense that Amal is 'on the house' – the occasional weekend we get without him when he has a sleepover at the Respite Centre. Sangi's leaving after school for an environmental studies field trip to some famous pond in Yorkshire. Time alone with Jas. I've got some fences to mend, no doubt about that. I'm sure the mutual love is still there, it's just under some strain. I do need to cut back on the booze. The clubhouse episode was a big red light. It's no longer as easy as I thought. I tried stopping midweek for a couple of days and felt like shit warmed up. The headache was terrible.

I'm still nowhere on the *Happiness Meter,* that's the fundamental problem. If I can't find it, I guess I'll just have to start faking it. The sheer injustice of what I've done to Tom Andrews continues to live with me, I can't shake it off, or cast it away. I can't progress as a Sikh, I can't undo what I've done, I can't confess and plunge my family into the abyss. I'm giving to charity now, but I can't tell Jas that most of it is going to the Salvation Army. Coming from our culture, that would just seem weird.

Typical these days, the week-end will have to start tomorrow. Jas is tied up with a tournament all day and then there's their annual summer barbeque to follow. I was invited, of course, but her club is several rungs up the social ladder from mine and I'm fed up with the Hooray Henries and their spoiled wives. I keep up the pretence of enjoying my own golf, but the truth is I missed the game with Dave Taylor and I haven't played since my initial debacle. Tomorrow, I've promised to take her for lunch and shopping in Birmingham. We both want to see the fabulous new library and the promise of that was enough to win me today's Get Out of Jail Free card.

I admire her through the front window as she climbs aboard her beloved Audi Cabriolet. She looks every inch the rich man's wife in her immaculate tennis dress with the white angora cardigan slung carelessly over her shoulders. I'm about to turn away when I spot the gates opening at the far end of the drive. A vehicle appears, it's a beaten-up Peugeot 307. *Shit – Balkar!* Go on Jas, get going! But she doesn't. She waits for him to park alongside her and she gets out of her car.

My heart sets up a tattoo against my chest wall. We've not met since that night in Ma Pardoe's; I've had no wish to. Seeing him is going to feel like committing the crime all over again. But now I'm left with no choice. They're talking together. It's going on and on and on. What the *fuck* are they finding so interesting? He's not *telling* her, is he? No – why on earth would he do that? *Go on,* Jas, you're late already! But still they talk. He's flirting with her now. I *know* Balkar; once a ladies' man, always a ladies' man. I have no fears on that score: his macho style amuses her, and repulses her, in equal measure.

At last! Jas is climbing back into her car and he's heading for the front door.

I move off to receive him.

"Hello, stranger," he says, grinning from ear to ear. "I've just had the pleasure of flirting with your beautiful wife."

"I know, I was spying on you both through the front window."

"And well you need to, young man! Beautiful woman, your missus. We both know she made the wrong choice. I was unknown to her then, of course. I told her from the beginning to divorce you and follow her heart!"

114

I match his grin. "You certainly did and she always gave you the same answer."

"Slowly, slowly catchee monkey – water on stone, water on stone. I'll keep working on it. I've just told her the same thing all over again."

"Come in, you silly bastard," I tell him. "Any marriage bells for you, any time soon?"

He holds his chin and looks mock-philosophical. "I'm in an extended period of appraisal."

"You always have been – but with how many?" We both laugh and I put an arm around his shoulders as we move into the lounge. "Same old Balky, you haven't changed a bit."

"Except I've got a whole lot poorer and you've got a bloody sight richer."

There's a definite edge to that one and it puts me on my guard. "I can't deny that. Sit yourself down, I've got a belter of a malt whisky for you to try."

"You always liked your whisky."

"Remember, we once planned a Scottish trip?"

"Great days, great days, but a man could be forgiven for thinking that he's been abandoned?"

"Nothing of the sort. It's been madness, Bal. First we went to India, to let Jas's family know. Then we were charging around looking for this place, then making it liveable, sorting the kids, feeling our way into a totally different lifestyle."

I pour the drinks with my back to him, not wanting to catch his eye.

"Different life, that's for sure. Just look at this spread! No forwarding address, Rakki, and your old mobile phone number just blanking on me? It's taken until now to track you down, and then only because I happened to bump into Isha's dad. Such a little scorcher, that Isha. Imagine having it with her?"

I fight down the offence I feel. Isha's a lovely, innocent kid. I can't help wondering whether he looks at Sangi in the same way.

"I'm sorry, mate," I say. "I know what it must look like, but I always intended to phone, just as soon as things had settled down."

"And me so loyal. Carrying around your guilty secret, with not so much as a whisper to anyone. And that not being worth even a word of thanks or the smallest of rewards."

He has my full attention now. "I trusted you, Bal, still do. That's why I confided in you."

"As I said: no thanks or reward."

Now, the emphasis is undeniable. "Is that what this is about, then?"

"Can you stand there and tell me it's never crossed your mind to offer me a lift up? You with the prize, and knowing that I'm still sweating my balls off in the foundry?"

I shrug and find nothing to say.

"The job that killed your old man and might yet kill me? The sad truth is, you've thought about it – and then done fuck-all. There was a time I'd have walked through fire for you, Rakki. You've let me down, big time."

"I've tried to explain. I always thought -"

"Driving over here, I wasn't sure whether to beg, or ask. Now I've seen you, I know it's neither. I'm bloody-well *demanding*."

"So it *is* what this is about."

"It's about *loyalty*, your loyalty matching my loyalty. You tight git!"

"How much?"

"Let's say two hundred grand, and that would seal my lips forever."

"You *have* to be joking!"

"I did some maths – it's less than five percent of the money you've stolen. Yeah *stolen,* Rakki. Anyway, like I say, less than five per cent. A few months ago, when you had no more than a hundred quid, you'd have been good for a fiver, surely?"

"The money's tied up, what's left of it. I'd need time. I'd have to take dribs and drabs from various accounts."

"My heart bleeds! See what I mean? Two hundred grand is dribs and drabs to you. It's not my problem how you raise it. You've got one month."

"And if I don't?"

I see something in Balkar's eyes that I've never seen before.

"Don't push it, Rakki. Rest assured, Jas would be the first to know, along with Sangita. I wouldn't stop there, though. I'd seek out the poor sod that you cheated, help him remember the Sunday morning Jas chucked him out. Then I'd make him an offer he couldn't refuse, there'd be sworn statements to the police. I might even see what the story's worth to the Sunday papers."

"You said yourself, the ticket's untraceable."

"Are you listening, man? You're trying my patience."

I pace the carpet, trying to decide upon a strategy. The bastard is sitting looking at his nails, he's actually *whistling.* I sit down heavily upon a chair.

"You'll get the money and that'll be an end to it – and everything that's ever been between us."

"Fine by me. But you've made sure that's happened already, wouldn't you say?"

He puts down his whisky glass, heads for the door and turns. "You'd better be serious, Rakki, or things could take a really rapid turn for the worse. You be sure to give my love to Jas, now, won't you?"

9

I sit nursing the whisky bottle. *The money you've stolen.* The words keep coming back. I've never actually denied it to myself – God knows I've had a heavy enough conscience. But when it comes out of someone else's mouth like that … I'm a common thief! I've layered it and insulated it with a million justifications about the good that it's done, I've even tried pretending to myself that my memory's faulty and that I actually *bought* the bloody ticket. Balkar's laid out the naked truth: I'm down there amongst the criminal scum and wide open to blackmail. It's an ill-gotten gain, always will be and I'll never know another day's peace.

The bottle seemed to empty fairly quickly, but when I check the watch I find that I've been sitting wallowing in my own misery for more than four hours. *This* is my only friend: the whisky. There's nothing to touch a good malt. I'm a connoisseur: there are dry ones, peaty ones, acidic ones, oily ones, each with its own distinctive flavour. Liquid passports to the Land of No Pain. If I was pushed to name a favourite, it would have to be the sixteen-year-old Glen Moray. Not *that* expensive as mature whiskies go, but the best forty quid I ever spend. I think the circumstances call for one, there's a couple stashed away downstairs. I rise unsteadily and wander off towards the cellar steps. Careful now, wouldn't do to fall.

The ice has gone: no matter; can't be arsed to go through to the dispenser. I pour a big glass and savour a slug of its tawny content behind my tongue. I think back to what Balkar and I had promised ourselves: the Speyside Single Malt Distilleries trail – Benromach, Cardu, etc. It wasn't a very Sikh-ish plan, but it's an enthusiasm we both shared. I tighten with anger. All over and done with! I serve myself another glass. The room's growing fuzzier by the minute and I'm feeling so fatigued. I might just take a little snooze -

"Rakesh!"

For a minute I think I'm dreaming of Jas shouting into my ear. It's very loud, feels less than six inches away. I almost fall off the settee with shock – it *is* Jas! She's standing arms akimbo, furious, looking down on me. It's proving impossible to collect my scattered wits. I try to rise, stagger and sit down heavily again.

"Wake up! Wake up, you drunken *bastard!*"

That gets through – that's *astonishing!* Jas has never, ever used that kind of language on me! She's shaking my arm like a madwoman.

"What? What? What?" I shout, rubbing an eye with my free hand. Angrily, I shake off her grip. I'm full of toxins and dopamine. I've been caught out – well and truly into my cups. *Why the aggression – what the Hell's got into her?* What time is it? Is she back early? I try to focus on her face and for the first time, I see that there's more than anger there, she's crying bitterly. It scares me sober.

"For God's sake, woman, what's wrong?"

She's choking on her words but they hit me crystal clear. It's *Sangita*. Jas has had a call from her group leader in Harrogate; she's in hospital after trying to harm herself! It's like being hit by an electric shock, or jumping into a freezing sea. I'm instantly wide awake, stone cold sober, totally focussed on the here and now.

"*How* – harm herself?" I demand.

"A friend heard her sobbing in a toilet and looked over the partition. She was sitting there with a penknife, she'd cut her wrists."

"Oh my dear God!" I'm on my feet now, close to tears myself. "Why? How? How is she?"

"She's stable and the cuts were superficial. They're keeping her in hospital tonight."

"Oh, thank you God, thank you! We've got to get there, Jas! We've got to go now! Oh my poor little girl."

She turns on me. "Yes and *look* at you – the state you're in! I'm finished Rakesh! I can't take any more of it!"

She lashes out angrily at the empty whisky bottle and sends it spinning across the room. "Go and put water on your face *and* change your trousers, you've peed in them!"

I look down, embarrassed, ashamed. It's true, they're wet and stained around the crotch and the worst of it is, I don't know if it happened in a drunken slumber, or if it was when she told me the news.

"Jas, I'll just be -"

"Stupid *drunk!*" she yells, "Now, I'm going to have to drive, the whole way!"

"Jas, please! We'll use my car, I can -"

"Don't talk *rubbish!*"

"Do you know the hospital? Did they give you an address?"

"I've got everything. For God's sake, go and clean yourself up!"

She is crying bitterly again, but it doesn't disguise the contempt in her voice. There's nothing I can do but hurry and obey.

The traffic is light on the M42 and Jas makes rapid progress around the Midland motorway network. I'm still wide awake and fully alert; the shock has nullified the effects of the alcohol. We're in my car, of course. We haven't spoken since we set off, I've let Jas concentrate on her driving. She breaks the silence when we join the M1. She's calm and focussed now.

"Do you think it could be anything to do with her worries about us? You know, all of that stuff she had in her head about us divorcing?"

I shake my head. "Unlikely, I'd have thought. I'm pretty sure I put that one to bed. She seemed completely reassured. Maybe it's trouble with school, or her mates, do you know where she is with all that?"

It's her turn for a shake of the head. "Only what I told you about skipping violin tutorials to be with them, but I think she's been OK since you spoke with her. She's been so happy since we moved and I've taken my eye off the ball. It makes me feel so guilty. I'm out such a lot of the time and I don't pay her enough attention."

"We ask such a lot of her with Amal."

"I know. But it has eased off a little since Sarah started and we got him his tutor. To be fair, you give him a lot of time too."

"I hope it's got nothing to do with that bloody Tony Pickles."

"Why should it have? It's not as though we've put a ban on him or anything."

"No, but you know what I told you: she was considering changing plans about the Royal College of Music to be with him."

She shakes her head firmly. "That was just a whim. She dreams of that college, Rakki, she's set her heart on it. I'm not sure that she's even seen him lately. They'll still be able to see each other in the holidays, anyway."

"Who knows? At that age everything seems dramatic and gets easily out of proportion. You think they may have fallen out, or something? God, why on earth do they have to grow up?"

"I'm so worried."

"Well, we'll find out soon enough."

Jas has speeded up considerably. It's difficult to keep the speed down in this car and we're doing well over ninety.

"Slow down a little, Love. At least, she's in safe hands."

She eases down.

"I shouldn't have had to do the driving."

"I know. I'm sorry, Jas, truly, I am."

"I meant what I said, you know – it had better be the last time I ever come home and find you in a state like that."

I bite my tongue. Even though I couldn't be any more in the wrong, I'm still Sikh enough to resent my wife's tone and the humiliation I suffered earlier.

"It was a one off, Jas, that's all. Balkar stayed late. There was a lot to talk about – you know I've not seen him since we moved. We ended up having more than we should have done."

"You *have* to cut down, Rakki. It's really worrying. You're regularly having more than you should. I don't know what's got into you."

"I know, I know. I will."

"I've heard it before, it had better be true."

"I've *said*; this has been a wake-up call."

"Bal seems to think that you've been avoiding him."

"He said that?"

"Well, have you?"

"God, Jas! What is this? It's turning into the third degree. I'll see Balkar again in my own good time!"

She takes her eyes from the road for a second to look at me enquiringly and we lapse back again into silence.

On the fringe of Harrogate I sat-nav 'Lancaster Park Road' and ten minutes later we pull into the district hospital car park. It's just after ten. I'm feeling sick and fatigued now – no food since lunch, Balkar's blackmail, a skinful of whisky, a row with Jas and Sangi's accident (I refuse to call it anything else yet). No wonder I'm ready to lie down and die. I've got no one to blame but myself. We hurry over to the main entrance. The minute we hit Reception, I get a lungful of hospital disinfectant, the adrenaline kicks back in and the headache disperses. Hospitals give me the creeps, but right now, it's my daughter that matters, nothing else.

Sangi's form teacher, Mrs Johnson, is waiting for us. She tells us that everything's *fine.* How I hate that bloody

124

word! I try to meet her smile of reassurance. 'Fine' is a relative term, it's like 'lucky' – when some poor bastard's lying in a ward with two broken legs, he's 'lucky' because let's face it, he could have been *killed*. Our daughter is alive and will recover, but she doesn't really meet my definition of 'fine'.

It's all true: Sangi borrowed the penknife on a pretext from a lad in her class and she's offered no explanation. The cuts are not too serious, the stitching will dissolve and the scarring should be minimal. There was no need for medication. She was calm and withdrawn and fell asleep quickly after the medical intervention.

Stop talking for God's sake! All I want to do is to see her!

We follow Mrs Johnson down a myriad of corridors. Everything's quiet, low lights are burning in the wards we pass. Sangi's in a little annex room of her own. We peek in on her. She's fast asleep with both bandaged wrists outside the hospital duvet. She looks a little grey under her dark skin but her expression is peaceful. I want to pick her up and crush her to me and tell her that Daddy will protect her from the evils of the world. I fill up and fear that the lump in my throat will choke me. Jas talks calmly with Mrs Johnson and the ward sister. We should be able to take her home in the morning. She's going to be – wait for it – *fine*. The sister isn't keen on us hanging around much longer. When Sangi wakes she'll be told that we're here to support her. We should come back at around nine in the morning. We say our thanks and goodbyes to Mrs Johnson after declining the offer of beds in the staff area at the field trip HQ and head off into Harrogate to find a hotel.

10

We're standing outside the ward waiting for the stroke of nine. These things are very regimented, you don't get in until the big hand is on the twelve. Sangi's sitting up in bed waiting for a visit from the ward doctor, who, we're told, is sure to discharge her. She hugs her mum and bursts into tears. I patiently await my turn.

"Whatever possessed you, Darling?" asks Jas, through her own tears.

Wrong question, immediately confirmed.

"Can we talk about it later? Please, Mummy."

I hold her long and tenderly and tell her that everything's going to be (I skirt the f-word) all right.

"We can go back to our hotel," I tell her. "We've left the reservation open, just in case."

"I want to go home, Daddy. Please can we go home?"

I drive. I'm bursting with questions and I know that Jas is too. We hold off on them. Sangi says very little, reclines on the comfortable leather of the back seat. I watch her through the driver's mirror. She looks troubled and stares out at the passing monotony of the hard shoulder. Jas and I make 'nothing' conversation and try to be inclusive in the banalities. We stop off for coffee and the three of us keep up the pretence that everything's *fine*. I'm relieved to get back in the car.

At the house, Sangi goes down first to embrace her pony. I'm almost at the end of my patience, but it's important not to push her into a corner. Finally we're inside. Sangi sits on one of the large sofas in our massive lounge. Jas goes over, parks beside her and takes her hand. I hunker down opposite to the pair of them, in a studio chair. The evidence of my stupid whisky-fest sits on a low table before us. The bottle that Jas clouted lies several feet away, under a window sill; it's the least of our worries.

"So, my one and only darling daughter," Jas begins. She's speaking Punjabi. She always uses it for terms of endearment. "I think it's time you tried to tell us what this is all about?"

Sangi begins to wail in earnest and would have wiped her eyes on the back of her bandages if it hadn't have been for Jas's intervention. We've never seen her remotely like this before.

"You know you can share it with us," Jas coaxes. "There's never been any secrets."

"My poor Darling." I add. "Let us in. I'm sure it will help."

"Daddy, Daddy, please don't be angry."

For no reason that I can explain, I feel a cold hand grip my spine. "What is it? Come on, Sweetheart, tell us all about it," I manage.

She is now barely audible and neither Jas nor I could ever have been prepared for her reply. "I think I might be pregnant," she whispers.

I'm on my feet instantly, like a rocket from a pad. "What! Who is he?"

"Rakki!" hisses Jas. She flashes me a look that could have downed a charging rhino and I collapse back into the chair. Jas turns again to Sangita.

"How do you know? Have you tested?"

I can't believe her *serenity*. Me, I'm ready to explode. Some *bastard* has ravaged my daughter, taken her virginity, left her pregnant while she's still a child! I'll kill him!

With an effort, I stay tuned. Sangi is saying that she hasn't tested, but she's two weeks overdue with her period. It's not a subject with which I'm familiar. I'm about to *disintegrate* – and Jas seems to be taking it all in her stride.

"So why ever should you jump to the conclusion that you're pregnant?" my wife asks calmly.

Sangi is sobbing pitifully again and it's making for hard listening. "Because Tony and I did it once, and when I told him about missing the period, he just got scared and walked away. He wouldn't even *speak* to me in Harrogate."

I'm on my feet again. "I'll give him *scared!* I'm going to find the little sod and wring his neck! Is he still in Harrogate? Is he?"

I *knew* it! Tony-fucking-Pickles has raped my daughter and now thinks that he can chuck her on the dump and run for cover! I'll kill the fucker, I swear I'll kill him and swing for it!

Sangi is crying piteously. "Daddy, please! Daddy, please!"

Jas is shouting simultaneously. "Rakesh! You'll do no such thing!"

For the second time, I collapse back into my chair. Jas cradles our sobbing daughter in her lap and gently pats her back.

"Look, Rakki," says Jas more calmly, "I think it's best if you leave us for a while."

She's making frantic silent sideways gestures with her eyes towards the door. I'm desperate to ignore her, but it's close to being a command.

"I'll take a tour of the garden – get some fresh air, try to cool down a bit." I rise to my feet. "It's not the last you've heard of this, young lady!"

An hour passes. I'm frantic to know what's going on, still angry at my exclusion, bursting with white hot rage at the little yellow-haired shit who has defiled my daughter. He's forced himself upon her, used and abused her and walked away! Furious with myself too – is it the dirty money that's heaped all of this misfortune upon us? Is it seeing me drinking and the two of us rowing that's driven her into his arms? Or is it living here in this godless country where my white neighbours think it's perfectly OK for their teenaged sons and daughters to fuck like rabbits?

Well it's not OK – not for the daughter of a Sikh! He's not just taken *her* honour, he's taken my honour, my family's honour. A daughter belongs to her family, her honour belongs to her family until she's married – then it passes to her husband to protect! It *has* to be like that, it's our tradition! I weep bitter tears as I stomp around the orchard. My little Sangita. Her future wrecked, her ambitions in tatters. I can't even *begin* to think what's likely to happen. I'm desperate for a drink, but it's more than my life's worth right now. I've got to fight down the feeling. It's true, me and whisky have become more than a casual relationship.

At last, at last, at last! Jas is walking over towards me. She motions for me to sit with her on a low garden wall.

"Tell me!" I demand.

"I'm not at all sure she's pregnant," she says.

It feels like a million ton weight shifting ever so slightly from my shoulders.

"How do you know?"

"I *don't*. But irregular periods do run in my family. It may be worrying, but it's far too early to say she's pregnant."

"But she said -"

"It's only happened once, Rakki."

"Once is once too many! I'm going to rip his balls off!"

"For God's sake talk *sense!* Get a grip!"

"Get a grip! A man's raped and impregnated our daughter and you say *get a grip!*"

"As far as 'raped' goes – they were alone in our swimming pool, they began to kiss. She confesses to having responded, having lost control. Before they knew it, everything's going on beneath the water and he's inside. He's a seventeen-year-old *kid*, Rakesh. He probably lost it within seconds – before he even knew. She says *she* didn't know – she found out afterwards, from the blood and his seepage."

It's the most horrible conversation I've ever had in my life! I try desperately not to form mental images. I'm

130

struggling for breath, temporarily unable to reply. My Sangita, party to *that* – willingly going along with it.

"What are we going to do?"

"I'm going out right now to get her a pregnancy testing kit. You're going to do *nothing*. We take it one step at a time."

I'm still having difficulty in believing that she's so matter of fact. Women really are a closed book to me. Jas is the one from the Punjab, brought up on all of the conservative taboos of our ancestry – not me! And yet it's *me* acting like some stereotypical traditional Sikh and Jas, the western liberal.

Jas drives off and I head back to the house. I'm not sure whether I should go and see her. I've no idea what to say. I love her more than life. I'd do anything to protect her from harm. There's no sign of her. I go upstairs. She's lying on her bed, her hands covering her tears. She sees me and cringes. She is terrified. My Sangi *terrified* of me; I can't deal with that.

"We'll find a way, Sangi."

The words have forced themselves from my throat and she responds immediately, a tiny glimmer of hope appears in her reddened eyes. She moves tentatively towards me and then throws her arms about my neck.

"There, there, Little One," I murmur and we hug for dear life.

"Oh Daddy, I'm so sorry." The tears begin again. "I just didn't know what to do."

"Could you ever believe that *losing* you would have solved our problem?" I whisper into her neck. Now we're both crying. We hold each other like this for some time and then I lower us both until we're sitting on her bed.

"It's been a shock, I have to admit," I say. "I'm out of my depth and don't know where we go with it. For me, you'll always be my baby girl."

"I've been so *stupid* – and now, I don't even know if I care for him anymore."

"He must be brought to account."

The fear returns to her eyes. "Oh, please Daddy, don't talk like that! I couldn't bear any harm to come to him."

"New territory for me, what to do next." I point to her bandaged wrists. "You're alive, that's everything. Whatever the outcome, promise you'll never feel the need to repeat this?"

She embraces me anew. "*Please* forgive him, Daddy. It – it – was as much my fault."

"I don't know what to think any more. I need time."

"Oh, I do so love you, Daddy. You're so honest and upright. I wanted you to be proud of me always, and now I'm so sick with myself."

She's weeping silently and we embrace again. The *irony* of it, the depths of my hypocrisy! Me, the role model – the upstanding benchmark of morality! I can see the disparaging grin on Balkar's face. I can hear the derisive laughter of the gods.

"I'll go and make tea," I tell her. "I'm sure we could both use a cup."

Downstairs, I grab a glass and quickly fill it from the vodka bottle I've hidden in the recess under the kitchen sink. I can't risk the whisky smell. I've just time to replace it before Jas's car reappears on the drive, she must have driven like Louis Hamilton.

"Just making her a tea. D'you want one?"

132

"Later," she answers. She holds aloft a Boots' plastic bag and heads for the stairs.

Once again, I'm superfluous to requirements. I pace the lounge, longing to go back to the vodka bottle. Far too risky. It's worse than the wait outside the maternity ward when Sangi was due for the world. I'm the spare dinner at the banquet. I don't know what the hell to do with myself. I try to remember a few traditional prayers for strength and fortitude.

After an age, Jas walks slowly back down the stairs. "No evidence of hCG," she tells me.

My face falls. "So, how bad is that?"

She breaks into a smile. "It's the pregnancy hormone – there's none – she's not pregnant."

I'm overwhelmed. I rush over and grab her in a bear hug. We waltz around the room, with Jas six inches off the floor.

"Steady, steady!" she cries.

"Oh Jas! Thank God you thought about testing!"

Could she be wrong? I put her down so abruptly that she almost topples over.

"You're sure?"

"Sure as sure," she responds. "They're pretty much infallible. She's had a lucky escape."

"That goes for all of us," I say, as I head for the stairs.

"Leave her for a while, Rakki, she needs time alone to come to terms with it all."

I turn and nod. Of course she does. I'm like a bull in a china shop. It's been a topsy-turvy few days and Jas is the one that came through like an experienced captain of a storm-stricken ship and me, the wretched (un)able seaman, spewing his guts out in the hold below.

11

I'm thinking about God this morning. Not surprising really I suppose, my mind is still in a whirl over our deliverance. I don't believe in the sort of god that you pray to and he intervenes, that's not the Sikh way. I've often thought how comforting that kind of god must be: you're in need of help beyond your own powers and capacities, you pray hard with due humility and bingo – God stops by and gives you what you want! If that was my kind of god, I'd be feeling pretty schizophrenic right now, singing his praises for Sangita and cursing him roundly for the pestilence of Balkar.

I don't have an old guy sitting on a cloud looking down at his children, nor a super being in his heaven dispensing justice to the deserving and punishment to the undeserving. If I did, I suppose I could expect the worst. I don't have a homocentric god at all. The Sikh God is the all-pervading soul of the universe, a power beyond knowledge to which all things conform and eventually, all things rejoin. We don't have holy relics of Him, symbols and icons for Him, pictures and tapestries of Him on our walls and we don't have smaller gods and angels and effigies standing in to help Him out. He's not even a 'He' or a 'She' at all: He simply *IS*. We Sikhs never did believe that we have all the truth, or even the vanity that our beliefs are in some way better than others. There are many routes to God and all of that is enshrined in our central teachings, but I suppose all faiths have one thing in common: you have to do the *right* thing for the *right* reasons – and it's as bad to do the wrong thing for the right reasons, as it is to do the right thing for the wrong reasons.

At school, I used to think the Christians were lucky. We learned that when a Christian confesses and truly repents, he can start right over again. The priest can even calculate how many 'Hail Marys' it will take. Because of Original Sin, no one expects you to *be* Christ – just to follow Christ's example. After each failure, you can truly repent, pick yourself up and start all over again. Maybe Christianity wouldn't have helped me that much? How could I possibly confess and start all over?

That's my core problem: confession would mean taking our new life away from my wife and family – and maybe prison for me. I've made my bed and I have to lie in it. As a Christian, I'd be condemned to eternal damnation as an unrepentant sinner. As a Sikh, it's not so different: my spirit is unable to pass the first stage and therefore in this life it will never climb closer to *Sach Khand* – the final union with the Universal Spirit.

My head is spinning now, but one fact remains clear: stealing the ticket was doing the *wrong* thing for the *right* reasons and it's cut me from my faith and driven me to drink.

Jas and Sangi are off shopping to Birmingham this afternoon. There's no point in Sangi returning to school before Wednesday as the rest of her class don't get back from the field trip until tomorrow. The three of us spent a quiet Sunday together, but today Jas feels like a little mother/daughter bonding. I've still not fully grasped how much my daughter has changed, but at least she's had the courage to be honest. I wish I could say the same about myself.

I'm going in to the shop. I feel a fresh surge of determination to stay at the helm. At the end of the day, it's the one single factor that has given me back some feelings of self-worth – the old Rakki, the happy-go-lucky guy behind the counter. It's a partial answer, sticky tape over the shell hole, but it's more positive than surrendering entirely to drink. Geoff Richards is the unexpected problem: I can't do *with* him and I can't do *without* him. He's so solid. He's got everything at his finger tips and the whole team behind him. I sleep easier in my bed with the money rolling in, but the ultimate frustration is that I can't seem to get my nose into the business any more. I just need him to move over a little, to accept that I'm not entirely without ideas.

I kiss the girls goodbye and head for Stourbridge. It's less than half an hour and I enjoy the drive. What a car this Range Rover Sport is! As with all of my new toys, I have difficulty in believing it's mine. I switch on a pre-programmed Country and Western station and *Ruby, don't take your Love to Town* twangs through the sound-surround system. I'm feeling better already, banging my fist against the steering wheel to the beat. I'm such a sentimental git, this one always brings a tear to my eye. Poor bastard! A crippled Vietnamese War vet' with an unfaithful wife.

The shop looks good. Old Jim is outside, cleaning the windows. Monday's a light day, it gives them time to sort out a few fundamentals.

"Oh hello, Mr Basra! Nice to see you," he says.

"How's it going, Jim?"

"Very well. Just thought I'd use a bit of a lull to give the front windows a going over."

"You've got a real shine on them." I place a hand on his shoulder. "By the way, you should call me, Rakesh."

He shakes his head decisively. "Oh no, that would never do. I'm old school – the boss is the boss."

I feel embarrassed, unworthy. I suppose it's because I know I don't deserve deference. I'm a good thirty years younger than him too, and I don't feel like his boss anyway.

"Suit yourself, if you feel more comfortable with that." I give him a reassuring smile and pass through the doors into the shop.

Isha's greeting couldn't be more different. "Rakesh!" she cries from behind the till. "Where've you been hiding?"

I beam a greeting. "A lot going on, never seems to be a dull moment at home."

"How's Sangita? I must catch up with her."

Isha is a couple of years older than Sangi but they're good friends from her time at the shop in Netherton.

"She's great," I tell her. "She'll have to invite you over for a swim in our pool."

An unwelcome recent image rears in my mind and I struggle to banish it.

"Give her my best," she answers. "If you want Geoff, he's in the back office working on something special."

I wander through and get a friendly nod from young Dev. He's busy restocking the canned fish shelf.

'Something special.' I'm curious. What's my resident genius up to now?

The office door is open and Geoff has his back to me. He's peering intently at a computer screen.

"Boo!" I shout.

He jumps a full foot in the air from his seat.

"Oh my God, you nearly gave me a heart attack! Phew! It's you, Rakesh. How're things?"

"Couldn't be better," I lie. "And you're still making me a fortune, then?"

"Doing my best. Just working on a fully computerised stock control system. I bought the software by mail order. To get it up and running I'm having to go systematically through every single item we have in stock."

"Sounds like a big job?"

"Big enough. I've been putting in an extra few hours each night. I should be finished by the end of this week."

"You must have paid for the software, then?"

He looks at me sheepishly. "It was a hundred and thirty quid, Rakesh, but it's going to revolutionise our purchasing and should save us thousands, long term."

"I can't have *you* paying for stuff like that. If it's about business improvement it will be VAT and tax claimable. I'll give you a cheque."

"Hope you don't mind? It was a bit presumptuous and I was quite happy to pay. One day I'll have my own business, so this is all sound experience."

"I'll pay you for the extra time too. Add up what it's taken. You're not being fair to yourself."

He breaks into a proud smile. "Well, I'm really grateful. But you really don't have to."

"How about we have a tiny whisky, just to celebrate our new stock control system?"

I can see he's surprised, but I've such a craving for a drink. I'm like a bear with eczema looking for a tree. It's the first time it's come over me, out of the blue like this.

"Thanks, but no thanks. I'd never be able to carry on with these inputs."

"Did you buy in the Glen Moray?"

"Two cases, like you said." He looks embarrassed. "They're all still on the shelf. At thirty eight quid a bottle, I can't see them selling around here."

"No matter, no matter. Fetch me one through. Surely I can have a little drink with my manager?"

He pulls a reluctant face but disappears into the shop. He returns with a bottle and two glasses, also from stock.

"Shall I use these?"

"They'll be fine."

"You'll have to forgive me, Rakesh, if I just cover the bottom of my glass – I'm not really a whisky drinker."

"Me neither. Special occasion!"

He pours and I feel myself salivate. He's taking far too much time. I take the bottle from him and top mine almost to the brim. He puts his hand over the top of his own tiny measure.

"Cheers!" I say. He chinks glasses with me. I down half the glass and smack my lips appreciatively. "You've got to admit, that's a very special taste, Geoff?"

He wrinkles his nose. "Must be an acquired one. I'm a lot happier with Banks' Bitter."

"That's my poison too. As I said, today, I'm toasting my first-class manager."

I re-top my glass. He looks ill at ease. We don't know each other that well and the atmosphere in the tiny office is perhaps over-intimate. I've drunk almost a quarter of the litre in less than a couple of minutes. He must be thinking I'm going to see it all off. Somehow, I find it in me to cap the bottle. He looks immediately more comfortable.

"I'll give Isha the money on the way out," I tell him. "I'll cover the glasses too. You can keep the bottle back here for next time."

"Whatever you say, Rakesh."

"Can't risk messing up your till receipts, can we?"

He's growing more embarrassed by the minute. I've shown him a side to me that he was unaware of and I was unable to disguise the urgency behind my drinking.

"So you're enjoying life out there in the countryside?" he asks, by way of making conversation.

"I came over to tell you that I was going to be taking a far more active role in the day to day business. I thought you could do with the help."

"Oh we *can,* we can -"

I put up a palm to silence him. "I've decided against it, Geoff, the place is running like clockwork. I can see that I'd just be under everyone's feet. Once you get your new stock system working, the place will be almost running itself."

"No, no, no –" he protests.

I smile and shake my head. "Tell me, is there a section in the new data base: *Surplus to Requirements*? I guess that's where you should slot me in."

He's horribly embarrassed. It was a needless self-inflicted wound – the whisky talking, I guess.

"We'll be sticking to our Friday night scheduled meetings, of course," I say, partially to rescue the situation.

"Of course, of course," he gushes.

"And you know I'm always there for you at the end of the telephone."

"I do *so* need that, Rakesh. I can't say how much I appreciate your confidence in me."

We stand and shake hands. I walk back down the aisles towards Isha with a heavy heart and pull two fifty-pound notes from my wallet.

"This is for some stuff I've just purchased. Geoff will tell you the price. Split what's left between you all."

"Oh my God! Thanks, Rakesh!" she says.

I stand for a moment, stuck for something to say. It's so unlike me – the old king of the one-liners, in my Netherton shop days. She senses my embarrassment.

"Oh well, give my regards to your dad," I tell her and walk out to the car.

I sit for some minutes behind the wheel until I spot Dev staring anxiously at me through the window. He sees me peering back and waves sheepishly. I wonder what they're thinking? I feel more depressed than at any time in my life. I'm not Rakki – one of the boys and their best mate – I'm The Boss: a remote, rich geezer, out of their league, who owns all that they touch and who keeps them in a job. I don't belong. They're a close knit team. What on earth did I expect?

I'm in no mood to go home. I could go and fire off a few balls on the driving range but the whisky will probably impair my judgement. Who can I call on? I can't think of a single bloody soul. Honest people are out there, hard at work. Besides, I've bonded with no one since the move. Unlike Jas! She could call upon half the county! I'm driving slowly, aimlessly in the general direction of Bobbington and home. My heart's so heavy it's only my trouser belt keeping it from dropping out of my bum. It's Balkar I should really be thinking about – I can't leave things until he decides to come sniffing around again. What if he turned up and told Jas? I shudder involuntarily. I'm going to have to set up a meeting with Shorrock and Saunders, the smoothies in Birmingham who look after our investment accounts. What will they think when I tell them I want to withdraw two hundred grand?

None of their fucking business!

I'm passing a big car park at the front of the Three Horseshoes and on a whim I give a last-minute signal and make a sharp left turn. The guy behind gives me a well-earned blast of his horn and I resist the temptation to throw him two fingers. I sit for some minutes in front of the pub, holding a noisy verbal debate with myself: *"Don't do it. You've had enough already at the shop. You can't risk turning up at home pissed – Jas will go into orbit.* I can hold my liquor and I can bloody well stop at any time! It's not Jas that dictates how much I can drink. God knows, she enjoys life and spends enough! If a bloke can't have a simple drink – *You know it's been getting out of hand. Look at the way you let down the family on the night of Sangi's emergency. Just suppose that there was another emergency when you get back? It would be the*

143

final straw. Jas has been pretty patient, all things considered.

I hit the steering wheel savagely and really hurt my hand. I'm perfectly capable of having just one for the road. I'll go and prove it! It'll break up the afternoon and there'll be less time to wait for the girls when I get back. Settled! I get out of the car and head for the entrance.

I find a window seat and sit behind a pint of Banks. It's bloody Geoff's fault; why did he have to go and mention Banks' Bitter? It just glides down, with that beautiful malty after-taste. I'm thinking about my old shop and how happy I was with the 'riff-raff' as Jas called 'em. There was always an overhanging shadow, of course: *I* was happy, Jas detested it. And now, out there in the leafy lanes, the situation's all but reversed. I return to the bar and order up another pint. This time I add a whisky chaser, it gives the drink more bite.

The place is quite busy: builders with their bum-cracks smiling out of the top of their jeans – talking football, OAP's clucking on about the kids of today not having any idea about hard work/the value of money/respect for their elders/sticking to a job/serving their country, middle-aged matrons with blond rinses and cheap tracksuits complaining about the latest bastard that's exited their lives, one or two gaming machine addicts, young, gaunt-faced and balefully focused upon beating the odds, half a dozen loners, spread thinly and staring into the middle distance, engaging in silent mental conflict with whatever irreparable calamities have blighted their lives.

What a rum lot Black Country folk are! When the railways first opened up the area, outsiders were appalled at what they found: a blackened land of smoke, ash and industrial devastation where no birds sang and the sunshine seldom pierced the leaden haze. Travellers told of a coarse, unlettered race who lived and worked in small sweat shops, bashing metals around the clock to form ships' plates and chains and all manner of industrial components that built the Great British Empire. Small furnaces lit up the night sky from every street and alley and work continued even during the sparse dinners of bread and yeast scrape that they ate, purchased from the dregs of beer barrels. Queen Victoria was said to have been so visually offended by the abject poverty and toil that she would close her rail-carriage curtains between Birmingham and Wolverhampton.

I order another beer and chaser. By natural selection, the folk around me are the Darwinian offspring of those early factory slaves. Raw, tough, long suffering and hard drinking. They know that life is no bed of roses, even though by comparison, they live today in a land of milk and honey. I smile at a recent memory and sit there reliving it. I was up on the Wrenner, our local sink estate, visiting Greg, an old schoolmate who's fallen on hard times. More to the point, he was fresh out of nick. He's a fellow shop-keeper and he'd done three months' porridge and lost his shop over a fairly sizeable VAT fraud. Anyway, there he was, jobless and living in temporary council accommodation. The street is one that's reserved by the borough for no-hopers: the ex-cons, the druggies, the unemployable, the evicted rent dodgers and those who have been kicked out of more desirable council properties for antisocial behaviour.

His semi is on top of a rise overlooking the main Dudley-Wolverhampton dual carriageway. We had a mug of tea and I dropped him a few quid and was just saying my goodbyes when I noticed two little kids standing on the bank with a handful of square plastic road-signs that they'd clearly pinched. They were the compact ones saying: 'No Parking' or 'Waiting Time Restricted to the Hours of blah, blah, blah.' etc. To my horror, the lads were skimming them like Frisbees across four lanes of moving traffic. Any time soon, one of the flying missiles was going to penetrate the windscreen of a vehicle and decapitate the driver at a contact speed of fifty miles per hour. I thought I'd seen it all, but then I spied their accomplice – a kid of no more than six years old – running between the moving traffic, across the four carriageways, to retrieve the spent missiles and to recycle them to the two older boys on the bank. It was more than my sense of public duty could ignore.

"Whatever you do, don't draw any attention to *my* front door!" said Greg, as I made a hasty exit from his lounge. "They'll come back to kick in my bleeding windows."

I walked up quickly towards the two lads, one aged about ten and the other eight. They hardly gave me a second glance, as they continued their Olympic endeavours.

"Listen, fellas," I began low key. "Do you realise what could happen if one of those things went through a car windscreen?"

"What's it gorra do with you?" enquired the older of the two.

The eight-year-old was more enterprising. "Gorra fag, mate?" he demanded.

146

In the meantime, the six-year old had miraculously arrived unscathed from the speeding traffic lanes and was redistributing an armful of plastic.

I toughened up. "Listen, stop what you're doing *now*, or I'll get the coppers on to you!"

"Fucking hell, mate!" said the aggrieved elder spokesman. "Can't we just have a bit of fun?"

"Spoilsport!" said his little lieutenant. And with that, they sauntered off with the replenished arsenal.

I thought that was an end to it, but as I turned away I heard a voice directed towards me from one of the nearby gardens. I looked around and saw an elderly gent sitting sunning himself on an battered tram seat.

"What was that?" I asked.

He drew heavily upon his pipe. "I *said,* Hey, Ali Baba, why don't you go and pick on somebody your own size?"

I thought for a second about explaining my public spiritedness, but the Union Jack was fluttering proudly from an upper window and I realised that I would be wasting my time. No doubt he'd seen the entire episode anyway.

"Thanks for your kind support!" I told him.

He had a parting word of advice. "Go jump on your magic carpet and fuck off back to Arabia!"

It was the turban obviously. It has that effect upon a certain species within the Wren's Nest. Actually I'd detected a slight Liverpool accent, so the chances are that *I* was more Black Country than he was. I felt like having the last word so I walked up to his garden gate.

"Actually, Dad," I told him. "I'm Aladdin's evil Uncle Abanazar, so you just be careful I don't rub my lamp."

I walked off appeased, even though my words had probably failed to register either culturally, or intellectually. There were one or two like him at my school in Netherton – the highest compliment they ever paid me was to reflect: 'If they wuz only orl loik yow, Rakki.'

The crazy thing about the Wren's Nest is that if you *Google* it, you'll find that it's a world famous fossil site. There are literally millions and millions of trilobites to be found. Over time it's played host to at least two tropical oceans, so I guess in its present phase, it can easily accommodate a few Sikhs amongst the rough and ready natives.

I check the watch. Can it really be two hours since I walked in? The clientele has changed. It's early evening drinkers now: the careworn on their way home from work, furtive couples having an illicit bit on the side after office hours, lads tanking up before going to the match. I need to get another one in. I've been backwards and forwards a few times but now I'm a little unsteady on my feet. I bash against the adjoining table – I'm sure it wasn't sticking out before?

"Sorry, sorry," I say to the couple sitting there.

Some of the guy's beer has spilled and his missus has a face like a smacked arse. I offer to get in a replacement for him but he totally blanks me. *Miserable bastard!* Same thing happens at the bar – can't seem to catch the landlord's eye.

"Hey, can I -"

I think you've had enough, mate," he tells me.

I can hardly believe my ears! "I'll be the judge of that," I tell him, with some dignity.

"No, mate, in my pub, *I'll* be the judge of that," he answers.

"Bloody racist!" I say.

Where did that come from? Must have been my earlier musings on the Wrenner. I simply never think in those terms.

"Don't pull that card on me, my friend," says the landlord, with justifiable anger. "I've got a ten foot Jamaican son-in-law out back. D'you fancy arguing the toss with him?"

"It comes to something when a man can't have himself a quiet drink," I mumble, deflatedly.

"Just go home, Pal. Go and have your quiet drink there."

I turn and concentrate my attention on the exit. It's suddenly incredibly important to walk a straight line. *No way* am I going to lose any more face in this shit-hole. I stumble a couple of times and bump into the door. No one noticed, I'm sure.

It takes me a while to find the Range Rover. It was parked out back, I think, but it's now on the front car park. I'm still angry – denying a guy a drink like that! I start the car. I know it's a right turn, that's the way out of town towards home. I've not gone more than a couple of hundred yards when the car gets a will of its own. Whoops! I'm running along the pavement. Back on the – too late, a lamp-post has appeared out of bloody nowhere! There's a terrible crash and a grinding noise from underneath, before the car finally comes to a halt on the grass verge.

I'm amazed the airbag didn't go. I'm in a panic now. If anyone comes, this doesn't look good! I slam into reverse and hear the wheels spin: I'm going nowhere. Four-wheel drive! I need the four-wheel drive! *Shit,* the wheels are still spinning, useless bloody four-wheeled drive! I'm stuck fast and going nowhere. The panic's stimulated another problem: I'm in real danger of peeing my pants. I'm not sure how much longer I can hold. I climb down from the cab gripping my crotch and risk a quick glance under the chassis; it's the bloody lamp post, jammed tight, holding the vehicle like a clamp! That's it – can't wait another second! I unzip frantically and pee into the kerb beside the car. The release is heaven.

Shit! Of all the luck! There are blue lights coming fast down the opposite side of the street. He's on a call to be in that much of a hurry? I try to stop mid-stream, but my bladder's not having any of it. He's clocked me and slammed on his brakes! He must have eagle eyes, the speed he was going? I'm facing a public indecency charge. Now he's reversing back down the road towards me. I zip up quickly. Stupid of me, of course he didn't spot me taking a leak – it's the Range Rover sitting on top of the smashed lamp post that's upset him.

12

It's ten o'clock before Jas is allowed to take me home. According to the copper who processed me, I'm looking at a two year ban and a fine of up to five grand. If I'm really unlucky, I could go down for up to six months; he thought that unlikely, as there were no injuries or third party involvement. The second cop in the patrol car was really savage. He was all for throwing in: 'an offence against public decency' charge, but the sarg' at the station must have taken pity on me.

I'll be a convicted drink driver. God knows how I'll manage without a car. We live in the middle of nowhere and I can't see Jas rushing to do me any favours. She hasn't spoken to me so far. The storm's going to break when we get home. To be fair, I'll deserve everything she throws at me. I'm a total and utter prat and on the road to nowhere. I feel so depressed I could just top myself and leave her with the money; at least she wouldn't have to walk around with my conscience about spending it. Not even Balkar would be shit enough to try to extort from my widow.

We sit down with a coffee. She's as hard as flint. It's a cold anger, well-matured from the hours spent waiting for my release and all the more deadly for it.

"Where's it going to end then, Rakesh?" she demands. "You're a George Best!"

"How d'you mean?" I stall.

"I *mean* what comes next: drink yourself to an early death from liver cirrhosis? Die of a seizure? End up in the madhouse with early Alzheimer's? Kill yourself and your family behind the wheel?"

"Jas! You know none of that's going-"

"I know *nothing* anymore!" She's sobbing now. "Except that once I had a *husband* – he was happy, witty and my best friend. Now I've got a miserable drunk! A man who makes promise, after promise, after promise about it and does *nothing!* A man who – let's be honest – can't even be a full husband these days!"

Even given the magnitude of my sins, I'm shocked at the unprecedented attack upon my manhood; I can't imagine the depths of her bitterness.

"On that last point, I think it's -"

"Well it's *true,* isn't it? Or are you going to tell me it's not the whisky?"

She's given me an opening. I could just confess the whole thing, tell her what's *really* driving me down. I haven't the heart. I'd be throwing out the baby with the bathwater. God knows where it would lead.

"I'll change. I swear it this time, Jas. No more drinking, you have my word of honour."

She's calmer now, as if settled into the base of her despair.

"Oh, Rakesh. You're such a *fool.* Do you really think that it's down to your *honour?* Do you really believe that you have the power within you to make such a promise?"

"Of course! Is my word *nothing?*" I thunder. "I've always told you that I could stop whenever I want!"

"You're sick, Rakesh. Can you not come to terms with that? It's a *disease* – a disease called alcoholism!"

"I don't think -"

"Unless you begin to accept that, I don't know where we can go with this. I've really had it! I don't know what to do any more."

She begins to cry, huge, pitiful, racking sobs and I know I'll not be welcomed if I go over and try to comfort her.

"OK, OK. Maybe you're right. I'll get some help. I'll do *anything!* I love you, Jas. I don't want it to be like this."

She squints at me through her tears with maybe just the tiniest glimmer of hope. "What, then? What will you do?"

She's going to press this hard. I'm being driven down a road I'm very reluctant to take, but desperate times need desperate measures.

"You've heard of Alcoholics Anonymous? I'll find a branch. I'll go along and see them, see what they can offer."

"So what do they do?"

"I don't know exactly, but they help you. It's voluntary, people join it to get off alcohol. It works – they're very famous for curing people. I'd have to find out."

"And you promise you'll do that?"

"I'll do it."

"When?"

"It could take some time. I'll have to make enquiries."

"It has to be *now*, Rakki. I'm not waiting, I mean it. I'm going on the Internet. If there's one around here, you're going – you've promised."

I nod reluctantly, confirm the name again and she takes off, upstairs. Twenty minutes later, she's back wearing a look of weary triumph.

"I found out all about it. There's a branch in Dudley, they meet at seven thirty on Tuesdays. We'll drive over tomorrow night."

13

We're sitting in Jas's car outside a large half-timbered building in Ednam Road, in the middle of Dudley. It's clearly a council building, as there's a big blue council board outside with gold lettering informing the public of what goes on in there during the day. On Tuesday nights it belongs to the local branch of Alcoholics Anonymous. Jas phoned the contact number first thing this morning, they're expecting me, there's no escape.

I make one last half-hearted effort to wriggle off the hook. "I'm still not sure I need it, Jas. Since the accident I've really had time to think and now, I'm feeling very determined. Maybe I can just stop of my own accord?"

Her look says everything.

"OK, then I'll give it a try."

It's seven-twenty and a smattering of men and women are beginning to trickle in. They're all ages, shapes and sizes and I notice there's even a few Asians amongst them.

"Bloody hell, it looks popular. You're sure it's the right place?"

Jas nods emphatically. "It's there all right. It just shows how many people need help."

I still can't think of myself in that way. I'm not really an alcoholic. I've been bloody stupid, that goes without saying, but I'm a guy with *backbone*. If I wasn't in such a corner with Jas, I'm sure I could just take some time out and deal with the booze. The guilt's something else.

"OK," she says, "Ask for Jack Daniel, he's the chairman."

In spite of everything, I laugh out loud. Jas searches my face for signs of an impending mental breakdown.

"What's so funny?"

"You can't be serious. It's the name of the founder of a great American whisky!"

Jas doesn't see the joke at all.

"Jack Daniels!"

"Look, Rakesh, I've had it up to *here.* Shall we just drive away and you can do what the bloody hell you like with your life?"

Big mistake. "I'm sorry. Really. I *am* serious about it."

Her face is a mask. "You'd *better* be. I'll be back at nine. He said on the phone that sessions usually last an hour and a half."

I lean across to kiss her but she quickly whips her head sideways. It's a painful reminder of just how out of favour I am.

"Go!" she says.

I open my door, swallow hard and head for Alcoholics Anonymous.

I'm shown to a plush office by a seedy-looking guy with nicotine-stained hands, who looks as though he hasn't eaten for weeks. He introduces me to the eponymous Jack Daniel, who by contrast is chubby, hale and hearty. He's sitting behind a huge desk and gets up immediately to greet me with a smile and a handshake. Name swapping over, he motions me to a chair on the other side of the large office and comes over to sit beside me.

"Ignore the office," he says with a grin, "I'm not nearly that important. I'm just camping; it belongs to some council bigwig during the day. Can I get you a cup of tea, Rakesh?"

I tell him I'll have it strong with two sugars and he moves to a kettle and tea-set located on a nearby table. There was a slight tremor to my voice. I'm surprised at how nervous I feel. He returns with the tea.

"It was your wife I spoke to then, Rakesh? She sounds a very nice lady," he says by way of an ice-breaker.

"The best. It was Jasvinder who thought that I needed some help from you."

He raises an eyebrow slightly. "And what do *you* feel about that?"

"It's been pretty bad lately, I suppose. I crashed the car the night before last. They're saying it was drunk driving. I'm going to get done for it."

"And was it?"

"I suppose it was really."

"So, the question is: do you feel that you're here for your wife, or for yourself?"

"That's a moot point. I guess I haven't really decided."

"It's the *key* point, Rakesh. This is a supportive network. It can only work for you if you're not in denial. You'll get all the help we can give, but at the end of the day *you're* the one that walks the walk, you and you alone."

"So, where do I go from here?"

"We'll chat a while longer, then if you feel ready, I'll introduce you to one of our long-term members to chat some more. If you arrive at the very personal decision that you want to help yourself, he'll become your sponsor: a kind of anchor man to support your progression."

"Sounds OK by me."

"So, what do you know about us?"

"Not a lot really – simply that you help people to come off alcohol."

"That's about the size of it, though I'd put it slightly differently: we help people to help themselves to come off the booze. There are no professionals here. We do get speakers in from time to time, but in the main, it's all about self-help and helping each other. We've all been there – looking at the world through the small end of a glass – and we've all had to face up to the same decision that lies in front of you."

I nod and sip at my tea, not yet ready to own up to much.

"At the end of tonight I'll give you a starter pack, so you don't have to try to remember everything you hear."

"So how long have you been going?"

"Here in Dudley? About twenty years. Internationally, since the nineteen thirties. In the early days in the USA it was more directly religiously-based, but in modern times it's changed to embrace all races and creeds. All are welcome, the only entrance card is the desire to stop drinking."

"Religious?"

"You don't need to worry about that. It had a strongly Christian beginning and we still believe that we need the help of an external power to make progress. The difference now is that you can use a power of your own choosing. There's even an Atheists' charter. You'll hear talk of the twelve basic steps that help us forward and the twelve traditions that help bind the organisation; they're important, but open to debate and interpretation too. Everything's very loose-knit and differs even from branch to branch. What holds us together is the mutual help and support. We swap experiences, we have an understanding of each other like only those who've been there can."

"And that must go for you, too?"

"Of course! I'm a reformed alcoholic who's taken some training in group therapy. When I say 'reformed', Rakesh, it doesn't mean I'm cured. Once you've been down the rocky road, the only way is abstinence. One drink and I'd be back on the bottle. I was a bank manager – the stress of the job got to me and I started having a few at night and one in the car before I got to the office. Then it was a few more at lunch time and one before key meetings. Before I knew it, I was incapable of doing my job, or anything much else for that matter. Thank God, like you I had a good wife. She stood by me and this place helped me to find my feet again. I'm a stationery salesman now, on a fraction of the money but much happier; I haven't touched the booze for four years."

I'm impressed. "So how long have you been in charge?"

He smiled again. "We don't have bosses, Rakesh. There's a committee drawn from our members, we look at stuff such as funding, organisational issues, external speakers, etc. I happen to be the Chair at the moment, but the positions rotate. You could even find yourself getting involved."

"And what goes on during the course of the evening?"

"Tonight's what we call a closed meeting. We do run occasional open ones too, when wives and family come along to a wider social gathering. In closed meetings we may run one or two formal activities, otherwise we talk in small groups and often one-to-one. We share our experiences of the problems that drink brought us, we listen and empathise with any particular hardship a member may be going through. Members meet with their sponsor – a more experienced member – and discuss their progress within the twelve steps. As I said, it's all about mutual support, developing the strength to keep to our non-drinking commitments. So, what do you think? Does it sound like something for you?"

"I'd like to go as far as meeting my possible sponsor, and I've probably taken up enough of your time already."

"Good! I'm sure you'll like the guy. His name is Tom, and unlike me, he really did lose *everything*. He's still living in a Sally Army hostel right now, but in spite of everything, Tom's a success story – he's been dry for several months and he's well enough to take on sponsorship. If you decide to stay with us, you'll be his first."

It's just too much of a coincidence! I've broken into a cold sweat. *Tom* – living in a Salvation Army hostel? There can't be too many combinations of Toms and SA hostels in the Dudley area? It has to be who I think it is.

"Maybe I'm being too hasty, maybe I'm not ready -" I begin.

160

"Meet him, Rakesh. That's the only way to find out. Chat with him now that you've got this far, at least see what you think."

Jack Daniel rises from his chair and walks out of the door. I stand and peek down the corridor after him. I'm so badly frightened my legs are shaking. I'm unsure whether or not just to head for the front exit as soon as he's out of sight. He stops before a door, grasps the handle and disappears through it. Too late, he's back out again before I can react. Tom's following him. It's Tom all right. From the brief glance I get, he's put on a few pounds and looks a lot cleaner and tidier. I duck back into the office, my heart still pounding.

I see the initial surprise on Tom's face: he disguises it quickly and extends a hand.

"Well, hello, Rakesh."

"Tom Andrews," I say. "How're things?"

Jack stares from me to Tom and back again. "You know one another?"

I nod.

"I used to buy cider from his shop – gallons of it," says Tom with a smile.

The statement makes me feel that I was complicit in a crime. "Only what you wanted," I interject. My reply embarrasses me, it sounds so stupid.

"Only what I wanted," agrees Tom, smiling even more broadly.

"Well, are the two of you happy to take it from here?" asks Jack.

I nod again.

"That's fine by me too," says Tom. "Let's get some more tea on."

"See you later maybe, Rakesh?" says Jack, "I'll go and catch up with the rest of the group."

Tom performs the same tea ceremony as Jack, then we get down to business.

"People said you'd upped and shipped back to India. It all seemed very sudden?" says Tom.

"We did. I'd inherited some family money – it came out of the blue and was enough to stop work and buy a property in the country."

"In India?"

"No, here, out near Bobbington. India was a holiday, a chance to see Jas's relatives."

He changes the subject. "So, has Jack given you some idea of what we're about?"

"Yeah, an overview, but now I'm beginning to feel a bit of a fraud. To be honest, my wife is teetotal, she can't stand my drinking and I came here to keep her happy."

He grinned. "The Old Dragon, as I once called her. Well, it's your shout really, Rakesh – either your drinking's under control, or it's not and you're in denial. Which one is it?"

I shift uncomfortably in my chair. "Well, it's not exactly under control, but I'm nowhere near to becoming an alcoholic."

"It's black and white, you know? Under control, or not under control? We can apply a little test if you like, are you game for that?"

"I suppose so."

"OK. Consider your answers to these questions. I'm not prying, so no need to answer out loud. Just think silently about your responses – how many would you be answering 'Yes' to? Here we go, then." He pauses slightly between each question: "Has your drinking caused upset and pain within the family? Have family or friends ever found you drinking and incapable during the day? Have you broken promises to yourself or to others, about stopping? Has your drinking ever prevented you from carrying out some important duty or activity? Has the drinking led to any violent incident, accident, or mishap? Have you ever considered suicide, or self-harm as a way out of your problems?"

He sits back and I realise that it would have been a 'Yes' to all of them. He doesn't need to ask, he can see that too.

"It's a sobering thought," I say. "Excuse the pun." It's a stupid time for humour, it simply underlines my discomfort. "So, it's true, I've got a problem. But I'm still *functioning*. I'm not rolling in the gutter, or losing track of days on end."

"If you gave yourself 'Yes' to everything, I'd say that you're past borderline. If you don't put a stop to it at this stage, then rolling in the gutter and losing days will be next. Beyond that, for many there are spells in and out of mental hospitals, liver disease and death."

"Magic! You don't exactly mince words, do you?"

"It's no joke, Rakesh. I've been much further down that road than you. Believe me, you don't want to travel it."

We're silent for a moment and reach for our cups of tea. He offers me biscuits and I decline.

"It's true," I admit, "I can't always say no to myself, these days."

"So what's been the trigger?"

"How d'you mean?"

"Well, it's relatively recent, isn't it? You always seemed a hard-working, sober kind of a bloke at the shop. You come into money – normally one imagines that makes for happiness and good times – but you begin to drink and within a relatively short time, it's at red-light levels. Have you come up with any personal insights into the reasons for that?"

This is bloody dangerous ground! This guy is *so* perceptive. I'm sweating again and my voice has a stammer to it. "Difficulty in coming to terms with the money, maybe? Complete change of lifestyle? I don't know – my missus has settled into it all much easier than I have."

"Women are more adaptable, up or down the social scale – that's a known fact."

"I *liked* the shop, I miss it, enough to have opened up a much bigger one, a supermarket in Stourbridge, actually."

I hope I've sounded convincing.

He switches tack. "Sorry, I didn't mean to put you on the spot, that's not what this is supposed to be about. I'm still new to mentorship and counselling."

"That's OK."

"Let's go back to basics. The initial decision: *I want to get off drink* – has to be yours and yours alone. If you think you've reached that point, then you join us and we offer each other mutual support. You meet the other

164

members when you feel ready, swap stories and become part of a tight-knit self-help group."

"I need it," I say. "You've convinced me."

He looks slightly worried. "That's not my role. You have to have convinced *yourself*, Rakesh."

"That what I mean – it's out of control. I've been in denial and I want to make the commitment, I want to stop!"

He smiles broadly. "Brilliant!"

We toast each other with the remainder of our tea like two conspirators.

"How about you?" I enquire. "Am I allowed to ask?"

"It was always the gambling first," he replies. "The drink came afterwards – first to celebrate my wins or to drown my losses, then when the losses became irrecoverable, the drink took over completely."

"You always struck me as an educated man."

"Educated but stupid. I was an accountant by training, but never practised. I was always very practical, very hands-on and I decided to go into property development – doing places up, doing the sums, selling them on. I made enough to buy myself a decent spread. My wife loved it, saw herself as the lady of the manor. Then the gambling began – first the horses. I had more money than sense. I'd graft until lunch time and spend all afternoon in the bookies. Later it extended to poker and casinos. Before long, I was remortgaging properties to cover losses, then finally taking out shark-loans. By then, I'd passed your stage of drinking. I'd drag myself out of the house in the morning and drink myself unconscious in some hotel room."

"*Fuck* ..." I comment.

"You could say that. Soon, the loan sharks sent in their heavies. It had to end. I threw my own residence into the ring on a crazy last fling and you can guess the rest – I lost everything. My wife knew about the booze, I hadn't been able to hide that. The first she knew of the gambling was when the roof disappeared from over our heads. She divorced me pretty much immediately. It's fortunate there were no kids. I don't think I could have lived with myself."

Sangi and Amal fill my mind, and I'm swept with guilt.

"And then you went to live at the Salvation Army hostel?"

"Much later. I was on the pavements for about two years. I even got to drinking methylated spirits."

"God, Tom, you've really been through it."

"That's what I meant about what you're risking. Don't go there, Rakesh. When I started using your shop, I'd just about turned the corner; I was on the slow road back. I had the Sally Army and a Birmingham rehab' centre to thank for that."

"But, you were still drinking at the shop."

"I'd weaned myself back to cider and the odd gamble on the Lottery, when there was a quid to spare. It was therapeutic, I thought – like the Slimmer of the Year having the odd cream cake."

Mention of the Lottery pulls me up sharp and reminds exactly to whom I'm talking. The feeling of guilt is all but overwhelming. I feel sick to my soul, wretched. This guy should be in *my* place, in my bloody mansion.

"And now?"

"It was wrong thinking. Total abstinence is the only way. Believe it not, your wife helped a little too."

I'm puzzled. "How come?"

"The day she chucked me out, remember what she yelled? 'Drunken riff-raff' It stuck somehow. 'I'm drunken riff-raff,' I'd say to myself. I didn't like the sound of it at all. It was as if it had pressed some button of self-awareness. Sounds stupid from the perspective of where I'd been, but there you have it. It's part of the reason why I came knocking on the door here and began the long climb out."

"I'm so sorry about what she said."

He laughs. "She did me a favour, Rakesh. I was at half-way house and ever since, I've been on the slow road to recovery."

"That's great, real progress!" Stupid response – I sound so patronising. "So, are you thinking of leaving the hostel?"

He bites his lip. "They'll be kicking me out soon anyway. You sign a fixed residential contract." He looks at his watch. "Bloody hell, that went quickly, it's nine – throwing out time."

"Thanks so much for tonight," I tell him sincerely.

"Are you coming back, that's the question?"

I shake his hand. "See you next week, same time."

"Read the booklet, though you'll soon find there's no substitute for talking things through with the other members here. In the meantime, don't think about 'giving up drinking' – think more in terms of: 'Today, I'm not going to have a drink.' That's the way we do it, one day at a time."

"Thanks again for everything," I tell him.

14

Sangita's pregnant again. I'm in a murderous rage, boiling over at the stupidity of it all. I'm standing in the doorway to our swimming pool, spying on her swollen, bikini-clad body. She picks up her violin, swings it in an arc and brings it crashing down on the hard poolside tiles. Fragments bob around on the water and Amal is screaming.

"No! Sangi, not your violin!"

It's the first time he's ever spoken!

I jolt awake beside Jas. I'm saturated in sweat and I can't stop my hands from shaking. *Fuck!* I need a drink so badly I could *kill* for it. The craving has all but chased away the nightmare. How long's it going to be like this? It's four o'clock on Thursday morning. I got through Wednesday dry, I swam, I mowed lawns, I mucked out the stable for Sangita. *A day at a time,* Tom said. It sounded so easy.

Maybe just *one*, just one tiny one would rid me of this terrible shaky feeling. I rise as silently as I can and put on a dressing gown. I'm half way down the stairs when I remember: I agreed with Jas to put all remaining booze in the granny flat. *Shit!* Jas kept the keys and I've no idea where she's hidden them! It was part of our deal. I lean over the kitchen sink, near to tears and close to vomiting. I'm not sure how much more of this I can take. I *am* an alcoholic, there's no denying it – to be suffering such withdrawal symptoms.

Before I left the meeting, Jack Daniel did warn me. He said that hallucinations, sweats and trembles were common in the first few days, but if my heart started missing beats, or I suffered any blackouts, I should get myself to hospital. It's difficult to imagine feeling much worse than this, but so far there's been nothing life threatening. There's a rustling sound behind me and I turn. Jas is standing in the doorway.

"Didn't think I'd woken you."

"You OK?"

"No, not really. Such a headache. Feeling sick. I had terrible nightmares."

"Oh Rakki, what *have* you done to yourself?"

"I know. But I'll be fine. They told me that the first days were going to be the worst."

"I don't want you left under any temptation. I'm going to take what's left out of the granny flat and destroy it."

"No need to go that far! Some of those bottles were forty quid each."

"Would you leave dangerous poisons lying around where Amal could get at them?"

"Well no, but -"

"So that's what I need to do to make you safe."

I nod resignedly. "Can you make me some strong black coffee, Love?"

"You don't want to come back to bed?"

"I'll be OK. I've got some accounts to look through, should keep me occupied until you're all up."

At ten thirty, I'm on an urban train from Stourbridge Junction into Birmingham Snow Hill and gazing at the mean little back gardens with their flotsam of decrepit garden sheds, fallen washing lines and broken plastic toys. It makes me feel how lucky I am, living in a mansion with its own extensive grounds.

I'm off to see Shorrock and Saunders in Colmore Row, to sort out Balkar's dirty money. Balkar's dirty money? What makes it any cleaner in my hands? I make an effort to change my train of thought – I need him out of my hair, then at least I can try and concentrate upon staying sober and being a good husband and father. That's not all, I've had an idea that's excited me: if I can find two hundred K to buy off Balkar, then the least I can do is to find another one hundred K to help out Tom! With that kind of money, he'll be able to forget about his hostel contract and set himself up in a small flat. Jas will be none the wiser, she's never once taken a look into our accounts and it will go a long way towards easing my conscience. As time goes by, if the shop profits keep rising and if he's happy about it, I'll be able to help him further. Despite the shit state I'm in, I begin to get a warm glow.

I walk out of the station and cross the road to the cathedral. What a power Christianity must have been in this great country! During all of the centuries that the peasants were living in tiny, stinking huts, they were building these great edifices to God. I walk past the graves of the great and the good who no longer care and wonder what issues they faced in their day. It's all over so quickly, and yet we get so worked up about it all.

The gleaming brass plate reminds me of where Shorrock and Saunders have staked their earthly claim and I walk in through their brightly painted blue door. A secretary hurries off to get appropriate refreshments for so important a client and Ted Shorrock walks in to shake me by the hand.

His thick bushy eyebrows soon shoot up when I tell him that I want to remove three hundred K from our portfolio. I know he's bursting to know why, but he maintains his professional reserve.

"You find you have insufficient flexibility within your existing liquid assets, Mr Basra?" he finally ventures.

"It's something like that," I tell him. Nosey bastard.

"It will cause some dislocation to the careful investment strategy we have devised for you," he adds.

"So be it," I say. "I'm sure you're able to suggest ways of addressing it?"

We talk technicalities. He wants to know whether I wish to maintain the current parameters of risk within the revised portfolio. He suggests the removal of this, the counterbalancing purchase of that, etc. etc. I grow tired of it, I'm gagging for alcohol again, but I continue to show deference to his professional expertise. Finally we reach an agreement. The deed will be done. He's going to start executing the arrangements immediately and the money should reach my nominated account within three working days.

He has one last try. "And you're certain you want to hold that much liquidity, Mr Basra?"

"Certain," I tell him. He's getting no more out of me than that. He's not my favourite type – plummy, self-satisfied, public school and Oxbridge no doubt. He's never managed to quiet hide his innate contempt for a brown-skinned nouveau riche. Too fucking bad.

The withdrawal symptoms are back big time as I make my way down Corporation Street and they have nothing to do with financial withdrawals. I linger longingly outside Wetherspoon's, salivating over the waft of stale booze each time someone opens the door. With near superhuman effort I move on and dive through the doorway of a MacDonald's. The double espresso tastes weak and watery, but it's hardly surprising when really, only whisky will do. It revives me enough to return to the counter for a refill and a Big Mac. I couldn't face breakfast, so I'm pleased to find that my appetite's not completely cut.

I wonder how the hell I'm going to make it through to the next AA meeting.

I nod off on the train and miss out on all of the sights that upset Queen Victoria. Back at Stourbridge Junction I have to think taxis. Jas agreed reluctantly to run me to Stourbridge but there's no return arrangement as she's playing golf this afternoon. We're still very much at the retribution stage of my fall from grace. I was wrong to imagine that the AA commitment and a couple of days of sobriety would win back all her trust. The taxi journey out to Bobbington brings home what a pain in the arse the driving ban is going to be. The Range Rover will be back from the repairers on Friday, but it might just as well be a Lego model for the next two or three years. Maybe I should just flog it? I feel depressed again and the sweats are back.

Liz, our cleaning lady, is at home. She tells me that Jas has left me a salad. I thank her but I'm full from the burger and go for the coffee again. The keys to the granny flat are back in their usual place on a hook in the kitchen and I'm curious to know whether Jas has carried out her detox mission. I take a walk over. Sure enough, the four whisky cases and the wider assortment of alcoholic odds and sods have been removed. I should feel grateful but I feel cheated. It brings on a dreadful attack of trembling and craving. If there was meths to be had in the garage, I think I'd probably down it like Tom did. I have to admire my wife's diligence: the removal would have taken several trips to her Audi to complete and by the time it was loaded, the poor car must have been well down on its springs. *What a bloody waste!* I wonder what she did with it all?

I sit down on the settee with the floral-design to collect myself. My breathing's laboured, but the trembling has lessened. I have to stop myself from visualising a bottle of malt before me. It's too much! I *have* to have a drink! *Fuck* AA, *fuck* Jas, *fuck* Balkar. Why in hell does everyone give themselves the right to interfere into my life! Gradually, I get a grip again. I concentrate on my surroundings. It's a nice room with a full outlook upon the garden. All in all, a great little unit, a genuine granny flat. There's a kitchen, a small bathroom with shower and toilet, a single bedroom and a sizeable lounge where I'm sitting. The place is kept warm and dry by a direct link to the main central heating. I permit myself a smile – Sangita's been pushing her mum like mad to let her move in over here. I can't see it happening; we both want her where we can see her, over in the main house. She has a huge bedroom to die for. Anyway, Jas still has ideas of her mother coming over to care for Amal. I can't see that happening either. We don't even cook Punjabi food and if the temperature dropped below twenty-five centigrade, she'd probably freeze solid and break into a million mother-in-law fragments.

Thoughts of Amal remind me that he's due back. Thursday afternoons are an early finish and Graham, the extra tutor we hired will be here to meet him. I stroll over to the house. The mother and father of all headaches has now kicked in and I set about finding Paracetemol. Crazy, but the booze suited me. I was never ill when I was on the booze.

Graham arrives before my son. He's a great guy and he's doing a fantastic job with Amal and eager to talk about him. Ill as I feel, I make the effort. For Amal, I'll always go the extra mile.

He thinks that Amal is making definite progress. "He's interacting more. Most of the sounds he makes are definite attempts at communication, Mr Basra."

I've noticed that too lately, especially when he's animated: around the flower beds, with next door's goats, or out at Halfpenny Green Airport. I say nothing.

"With his books too, he's been pointing to things recently. Before, it was difficult to get any focus of attention."

"They changed his medication at the last assessment," I reply. "I think that's significant."

"I've come across that before. Some of the anti-convulsive drugs are really hit and miss. Maybe he was over-medicated, or maybe one of the new drugs has triggered some part of his brain? It's early days, Mr Basra. Sometimes, with his condition, there's serious regression – but with others, there's sudden progress and they go on into adulthood even to manage sheltered, independent living."

"I know. We live in hope."

"If we could just get a breakthrough in communication. I'm sure the words are there. It's the key, you know, getting over the linguistic barrier would be the beginning of real interaction."

I let him talk. He's young and enthusiastic. I'm well-read on the points he's made, I've spent hours reading up on autism, but I admire his enthusiasm. I wouldn't have it any other way, it can only be for the good in his dealings with my son.

15

I've been dry for seven days. I have to pinch myself. It's been a struggle and there's been no instant leap back into rude and vigorous health. The excruciating headaches and the sweats have eased, although they return frequently enough to remind me that I've still got a long way to go. The worst side effect is a deep depression and without the car, I'm bored out of my tree. It sits mockingly on the drive and it's more than my life's worth to touch it. On three consecutive afternoons I've taken the bus to look in on the shop. I'm now an expert on local transport timetables. So much for being a millionaire! Jas makes no effort to offer me lifts and I'm not going to bloody well beg.

The shop hasn't worked out as my new purpose in life. I've had to accept that the dream is now dead in the water. Geoff is as super-efficient as ever, *damn him*. By way of compensation, the week on week rise on the takings is turning the place into a money milch cow. When I'm there, I try to fit in and bless them, they all do their best to look so damned grateful. Isha finds it difficult to keep up the pretence when I take over her till for a while. Her face says, *'You're welcome!'* and her body language says, *'Get the hell off it!'*

Most of the time, when I make self-conscious conversation, I feel like some visiting head of state. By contrast, I've no idea what they must make of me. I probably come across as a pathetic loner, desperate for human contact and maybe that's not too far from the truth? At least I haven't asked Geoff for the rest of the whisky: I'm keeping that unfinished bottle at the back of the shop as a trophy, something to be proud of and to remind me of my new found strength and resolve.

We're sitting outside the building in Ednam Road again. It's the one place where Jas will still drive me without question or argument. I have a cheque for one hundred grand made out to Tom Andrews sitting in my back pocket and I'm stupidly excited. The alcohol abuse was *meant* to happen, I can see that now. The fates conspired to bring Tom and me back in touch and I have to jump at the opportunity. Will he accept the hundred grand? It's a mere token of what he's owed, but it's a beginning. In my mind, I've expanded the idea: I want to pay him back in full. It will take time, I know – years maybe: I'm going to develop a string of supermarkets to feed the funds. I'll be like the Sainsbury Charitable Foundation. Why not? Everyone has to start somewhere. The thought gives me comfort. Maybe in the fullness of time I'll even be able to absolve myself and find peace, regain happiness.

I kiss my wife goodbye and she wishes me a good session. Tom meets me in the corridor with a handshake and enquires how I've been getting on.

"Dry," I tell him.

"What – ever since the last session?"

"Yep."

"Brilliant!" He's as pleased as Punch, grinning like a Cheshire cat. "That's pretty impressive! Cold Turkey's no joke. No room for complacency though. How rough was it?"

"Rough enough," I'm grinning like an idiot too. I feel like the kid who's just won teacher's prize.

"Let's go through to the office and chat a little more. Then, if you feel ready we can join in with tonight's group session."

I sit and wait whilst he goes through the mandatory tea making ritual. We settle into chairs with our steaming mugs.

"I told you, it's one day at a time. You've done amazingly well. I didn't make it to dry in my first week, nor in my second or third, come to think of it."

"You had a lot further to go than me."

"True, but everyone's battle is unique. The trick now is to know your trigger points and be on your guard against them – the thoughts, emotions, situations that might set you off down the wrong path again."

"Easier said than done."

He misunderstands, of course. "For example, you mentioned last week your difficulties in coming to terms with your new wealth? If that's an issue, learn to confront it: there must be times in your commercial and business dealings when you're particularly vulnerable? Or maybe it's times when you think your spending's particularly lavish? I don't know, but you get the picture? It's for *you* to pinpoint the issues and to be ready for them."

I nod to acknowledge I've understood. He's encouraged to continue. "I know this sounds like a bit of a lecture, Rakesh, but I'm trying to paint the landscape that you'll be walking through. At the inner level, there's almost certainly other unresolved personal issues: you may be acutely aware of them, or they might be lying beneath the surface. We're all different. The key is to hang them out to dry, to confront them. That's the point of the group sessions here, the more you feel you can share, the more of the baggage you unload. You'll listen to other people's battles, their personal triumphs and set-backs and hopefully, when you feel ready, it will encourage you to share your own."

"I've bleated on enough about the main one already."

"Coming to terms with the new life-style, accepting your good fortune over the legacy?"

"I'm a Sikh, Tom. Money and material wealth don't come easy, it's not the path to spiritual progression."

"That's a tough one. So there are no rich Sikhs?"

"According to our gurus I should be putting back into the community, giving ten percent to charitable causes."

"And you're not?"

"Some – but we're living out of town in splendid isolation. And then, in India, it was a shock to see so much poverty and suffering. It makes you feel that you've no right to such wealth."

"I guess your gurus have a point. It's probably a question of what you do with it?"

"*You* would be a good starting point. You're in difficulty at the moment, I'd like to help you."

"*Me?*"

"You told me that you're about to be kicked out of the hostel."

He looks uncomfortable. "Not exactly kicked out. I entered into an agreement and the term is up. They've been fantastic, but I'm expected to move on."

"And you've no idea where?"

"I wish I did, but it's a confidence thing right now. I'm not completely out of the woods. I don't know how to get started, how to jump back into the swim."

"I'd like to offer you a sum of money to help."

To my surprise, he laughs." A sum of money! You might just as well offer me booze!"

"I'm not with you?"

"I told you, Rakesh, first and foremost I was a gambler, a gambler from sun up to sun down. It was an addiction even worse than the booze. Even now, I don't know whether I can trust myself with money. In addition to AA, I'm a fully paid up member of Gamblers Anonymous. If ever the gambling kicked off again, I'd be back into the vicious circle that almost destroyed me: bookies, casinos, then countless hours on the booze, celebrating wins, or drowning my losses."

"But it needn't be like that. Think what you've been telling me about knowing your trigger points?"

"Exactly and I hope I'm winning the fight. I've learned to keep away from cash and say no to booze, but left alone with a wad, anything could happen. Ten pound notes would be more dangerous for me than full pint glasses."

"So, at least let me buy you a flat? I could pay your bills and you could carry minimum cash."

The atmosphere changes and his expression is now registering puzzlement and concern. I see in an instant that my enthusiasm has run away with me. I've offered a virtual stranger generosity beyond normal expectation. My guilt has blinded me and the solution I thought I'd found has the potential to raise more suspicion than gratitude. He confirms my fears.

"I'm not sure where you're coming from, Rakesh? You don't owe me a thing, I'm just one of your ex-customers? If you feel the need to give to charity, *do it* – there's a thousand and one noble causes: AA and the Sally Army for starters. Or what about the starving in India?"

Thank God I didn't pull out the cheque for a hundred grand. I can see the madness of it now – any sane individual would have reacted as he did. You just don't go around making offers of free flats to strangers.

"Of course," I agree, "and I'm looking at a number of worthy causes. It's simply that from where I'm sitting, there's a man who's doing his best for me. He's in dire need himself and it strikes me that I'm in a position to help him."

He's still looking very ill-at-ease. "Well, thanks but no thanks, Rakesh. The word *charity* doesn't sit very comfortably with me. I suppose I've had a bellyful of it since my fall. No disrespect of course, but it's so demeaning."

"I can understand that," I tell him. "I'm sorry, no offence meant."

"None taken. You're a genuine bloke."

The words grate painfully, particularly coming from Tom. We sit drinking tea. It's difficult to pick up again on conversation after so personal an exchange.

I don't know where it comes from, but I'm hit by a sudden brainwave. "Listen, I've had a thought – d'you drive?"

"I did."

"You kept your licence?"

"Still valid as far as I know."

"I'm just about to advertise for a part-time chauffeur. Why not you?"

"But I don't think I'm looking for -"

"*Listen,* Tom – I'm not talking charity here – I'm in deep shit. I'm facing a two or three year ban. Drive me around in my Range Rover and I'll pay you for it. The regular work could give you the springboard you're looking for."

He looks embarrassed. "I'm sorry, but when I leave the hostel, I'll have to rent somewhere, start paying my way. I probably need to look for something full time."

"You said you're a hands-on guy? I've got ten thumbs and there's loads needs doing to the place. I could easily make up the difference in hours. I need gardening help too, if you could turn your hand to it?"

"And that's on the level?"

"God's truth. I'm bloody desperate for assistance."

He seems half-tempted. "I'm no gardening expert, though I worked on my own place, of course. Anyway, it's a non-starter, you're miles away, out in the sticks."

It comes out before I've even thought it through. "There's a granny flat, you could bunk there. No strings, you just move on whenever you feel you're ready."

"I don't know -"

"Live free and I'll bank your wages for you until you feel able to deal with money again? Come on Tom, it's win-win! You get your own place, a chance to return to independent living and you don't have to worry about getting dragged back into gambling."

"You're a very persuasive man, Rakesh."

"Make no mistake – it's tailor-made for both of us – *and* you can help keep me on the straight and narrow."

"And what about the Dragon? What's she going to say about it all?"

I'd reckoned without Jas. What indeed will my wife have to say?

"You shouldn't call her that."

"I know. I'm sorry."

"She'll be OK. I know she can seem fierce, but she has a heart of gold."

"I'd feel a lot more comfortable if I knew she'd approved."

"Leave it with me and I'll talk with her. Give me the number for your hostel and I'll get a message to you there tomorrow."

We stand and he takes hold of my hand. "Rakesh, you're sure about this? Because from where I'm at right now it's just too good to be true, the best break I've had in years."

No doubt he still thinks I'm being wildly generous. If only he knew just how much in my own interest this is. It will go a long way towards mending me. I'll live with a lighter conscience and maybe shed some of my self-loathing. I feel the guilt draining from me.

"It would make me more happy than you'll ever know. It covers a lot of my trigger points."

He smiles at that.

16

Jas and I have the biggest row of our marriage. She is incandescent. I'm no macho-man or sexist – far from it – but sorry as I am to upset her, this is one argument I simply can't afford to lose.

"If he's riff-raff, then *I'm* bloody riff-raff," I yell. "Where's the difference? *He's* been an alcoholic, *I've* been an alcoholic. According to you, that makes *me* riff-raff! The only bloody difference is that I'm rich and he's poor!"

"If you can't see the difference, more fool you! He was rolling around on the streets, living rough, sicking-up on our doorstep, for God's sake!"

"He's a fallen guy, down on his luck and he's not touched a drop for a year. Huh! If only I could say the same about *me*!"

We fall into an angry silence. Finally, I try another tack. "Look, Jas, you're the first person to say that I haven't settled down. Look at the mess I'm in: unhappy, unfulfilled, unable to enjoy the money. Then there's been the drink. I want to *do* something for someone – to make a difference, to feel that some good can come from our good fortune – to people other than just ourselves."

"*Give* it away then! Walk down the street and hand out fifty pound notes."

"You know that's not what I mean. As a Sikh, I should be giving to charity anyway. This is a chance, a practical opportunity to help someone – to give this guy a lift up, back into being a useful member of society."

"And you have to pick the one man who came into our shop and openly insulted me?"

"But that's not *him*. I'm sure he's sorry. He's nothing like that. I've had the chance to speak with him – he's helping me, mentoring me. He's an educated bloke, doing his best now to find his way forward."

"And you think his rehabilitation should happen at our expense?"

"Not 'at our expense' as you say. Can't you see, we need his skills?"

"And in the accommodation I've furnished for my mum?"

"Be realistic, she's coming over no time soon. He'll be long gone by then and I repeat and repeat and repeat: he's *not* free-loading. He'll be looking after the property and relieving you from the problem of driving me around."

"That's what *you* say."

"I need him Jas. You want me off the drink. He can support me, he's already achieved that for himself. I'll make you a promise: if he doesn't stick to his side of the deal, then he's out, I'll have no hesitation."

She loses the argument. "Be it on your head then! I'm so fed up I could just walk out, catch a plane back to India! Why the hell can't you just be *normal?* Enjoy our money and be happy with our good fortune?"

We lapse into another silence and I know she's close to breaking down. I attempt to put an arm around her, she pushes me off.

"I'll say this only once, Rakesh: you keep him well away from me and my children!"

She storms from the room. I wait a while, take out my mobile and dial Tom's hostel. I leave a message saying that all arrangements are in place and I'll see him as usual on Wednesday evening. I'm totally convinced it's the right thing to do. If Jas only knew about the real origin of our money, she'd understand. I'll be a better husband and a better father from this, it's worth the current blow to her pride. I'm the man at the head of a Sikh household. If I let *that* go, who am I?

An uneasy couple of days pass. Fortunately, Jas is really tied up; she's now the rising star of her golf club and it's the week of the women's annual knock-out Club Championship. She's winning every round she enters and it's looking like she might make the final stages at the week-end. I moon around the house most of the time, once or twice, I make a search to see if I've left the odd bottle stashed away anywhere. There was a time when I was hiding them all over the place. I'm not really sure why I'm poking around. Maybe it's to lay down a challenge: look but don't taste? The craving still waxes and wanes and the ongoing tension between Jas and me doesn't help.

I can't wait to get Tom installed now. There's guttering and fencing to mend and doors and windows to paint. I'll be mobile again and out of Jas' hair! I begin to take a new interest in the garden. It's obvious that if he's up for it, we could get started upon a major renovation –

it's the worst feature of the entire property, with whole areas overgrown.

On Saturday, Jas reaches the semi-finals and we're all up early on Sunday morning to witness her greatest day. Tom and our differences are on the back burner for a while. She's completely focussed on the competition. For a woman of such strength and independence of character, her life in England has been pretty unfulfilling. I realise that apart from her secretarial job, this is the first time she's ever achieved anything of significance for herself. It means a lot to her and it means a lot to me too. Sangi and I are very proud of her.

The final is played over two rounds of eighteen holes. We dine at lunchtime in the clubhouse. The morning round went well and she's two shots ahead of her opponent. Over the soup, she tells me that her rival just happens to be the club captain.

"Maybe this afternoon I should just let her win," she says conspiratorially.

"You'll do no such thing!" I reply.

Amal is going through a grunting-out-loud stage and getting one or two disapproving looks. Well *fuck* 'em. If they don't recognise special needs, too bad. There's a black family sitting opposite, they give us a smile. Jas says that the woman of the family is a top surgeon in Sandwell. There are no other Asians but us, although Jas tells me that she does have one Hindu girl friend who plays.

"Not too much of a balanced ethnic mix," I whisper. But things are no different at my club. Is it that we Asians just don't play sports, or is it that we're simply under-represented in the top slice of society? I suspect it's the second – plus maybe a little 'selectivity' in membership processing at some clubs.

Five o'clock and Jas wins! Hey, I've got a celebrity wife! Her picture is taken for the *Express and Star* and everyone wants to know her. Even the club captain is graceful in defeat. The kids and I retreat into the background. It's *her* moment and well-deserved! It doesn't take a genius to work out that she's going to be even more strongly involved with her club than before.

17

On Monday and Tuesday Jas is still high on her win and we both studiously avoid the subject of Tom. I'm guessing that for the first time, she's not going to volunteer to take me to the AA meeting on Wednesday evening and I'm right. At seven, she sees me ordering a taxi and feigns surprise as I put down the phone.

"I'd have taken you, you know," she says, unconvincingly.

"No problem, I've ordered it now. Didn't want to bother you."

"Oh well, I suppose you'll have your own driver very soon."

"It'll solve a lot of problems. At least admit to that, Jas."

"Let's not open up that again! You've made your decision, but it goes without saying that we could easily have afforded a part-time driver and a part-time gardener, without you having to impose *him* upon us."

I should have known that Jas would have wanted the last word. Do all women end arguments with: '*I don't want to say any more, but...*'? I've found the safest response is a non-committal shrug and to hope that it ends there. On this occasion, it does.

I meet up with Tom at the Ednam Road building. We retire to the big office. It dawns on me that I haven't met a single other member at AA, just good old Jack Daniel and Tom Andrews. Does it really matter? I'm on the wagon and the new relationship with Tom has re-energised me. He wants reassurance about Jas. I have to be straight about it – he'll find out soon enough. I tell him that she's not the happiest bunny in the burrow, but that she'll get used to the idea – particularly if he can help out with giving the gardens and grounds a make-over. He doesn't look too happy and for one terrible moment, I think he's going to pull out. I have to persuade him all over again, but it's easier this time as he has a deadline of Saturday to be out of the Sally Army hostel.

"She still remembers the harsh words that the two of you had," I tell him. "In fact, all that weekend, she'd been having a really bad time. We'd had a bit of a falling out, then one or two people upset her and you just happened to be the last in line. What you copped was transferred anger. I was the real target. According to her, I hadn't been offering enough support."

He grins. "I remember the argument – you were distracted and she was getting more and more wound up."

"Distracted?"

"You were in the middle of checking my lottery ticket, remember?"

I go cold all over. God Almighty, he remembers the *lottery ticket!*

"If you say so. I'd forgotten the detail. Anyway, it was wrong to have chucked you out."

"Water under the bridge."

"The truth is, she was always unhappy there. We had petty squabbles all the time and then forgot them just as quickly."

"Wish I could say the same for me and my missus. After I gambled away the property, I think she dug out, indexed, filed and stored every grudge."

"Poisonous!"

I'm still shaking and hoping that it's not too obvious. He can't possible know anything about the ticket? It was just sheer bloody coincidence?

"My fault entirely – there was just too much for her to forgive."

"My drinking's certainly put our relationship to the test."

"Never been tempted with gambling, then?"

"No, thank God. The booze has been more than enough."

I'm hot one minute, cold the next, the stress is unbearable. Is he playing with me, or is it just my sickly conscience? I struggle inwardly to get myself together. I'm being ridiculous, paranoid. The poor guy has no idea – *can't* have any idea. I just need to steer us away from the entire subject.

"So, you're cool now about moving in? All doubts resolved?"

He nods and smiles. "I know I'm going to have to apologise to her for the 'dragon' remark."

I shake my head. "I wouldn't say anything for a while. The best strategy is low profile, gradual improvements to the property and grounds, me off her hands with you driving. She'll come around, it'll just take a little time."

"OK by me, I'll be discretion personified."

"You need to know that Jas is basically a lovely person. She's had this idea that her mum's about to fly over from the Punjab and live in the granny flat. To be honest, a flight of pink elephants will arrive before she does. She hasn't been out of her village since the anti-Sikh riots of nineteen eighty-four."

"Another reason for the resentment though?"

"I guess so – it underlines what Jas knows already – her old mum's coming no time soon."

We drink tea. It's agreed all over again now.

"Tell me what time you want a taxi to pick you up from the hostel," I ask.

"I can get there."

"We're in the middle of bloody nowhere, as you pointed out. Just tell me what time?"

It's early Saturday morning and Jas is off golfing already. Tom's taxi is due. I'm relieved there'll be time to get him fully installed and out of sight before she's back. It will take some of the heat out of the situation. Sangi is in Brum for her violin tutorial and I've got Amal for the day. I can't see how it's going to be possible to keep him out of sight of Tom. Jas is being unreasonable anyway. The guy's an ex-alcoholic, not some raving paedophile. I'll respect her wishes when she's around – which is less and less – but if he gets to know Amal, I'm not going to break a leg to prevent it.

The taxi's here. I've just finished opening up the granny flat, perfect timing. Tom climbs out with an old rucksack slung over his shoulder; I guess it must contain the sum total of his worldly possessions.

"Welcome!" I say, by way of greeting. "Jas is out golfing and this here is young Amal."

He shakes my hand and smiles towards Amal.

"About the same sized spread that I had," he observes, as I pay off the taxi man.

"Really?" I'm impressed, I don't know why. I suppose it's because it brings home to me the magnitude of his loss.

He grins. "I'm exaggerating. The grounds are similar, but my place was less than half as big." He bends forward towards Amal and ruffles his hair. "Well young fella, I saw you a couple of times in the shop."

Amal stands his ground and looks at Tom with his big brown eyes.

"That's a good sign," I tell Tom. "When he doesn't like someone, he looks at them as though they're something that's stuck to the bottom of his shoe."

We both smile.

"What condition does he suffer from, exactly?" asks Tom.

It's stupid but even now after all of these years, I hate it when people talk about Amal's 'condition' or 'handicap'.

"Autism. There's a chance he might get better as he gets older."

"And you like your new house, Amal?"

Amal continues to regard the stranger with a steady gaze and I wonder what's going on in that head of his.

"He knows what you're saying but he doesn't talk."

"And you say he might get better?"

"He's very bright, but he can't interpret the world the way we do – can't put himself in anyone else's shoes, so he doesn't know how to interact. The latest research suggests that we get to know the world by copying others, their gestures their emotional responses. Babies smile when they're smiled at, toddlers copy and imitate others in play. Autism places a filter in the way, so autistics don't pick up the clues, they live in a world of frustration because they don't fit in."

"So he's cut off from the world?"

"Not completely. There's a spectrum: at the mild end, people just seem a little odd and have some problems catching on, at the severe end, yes, they're cut off – in between, there are various degrees of severity. We're not sure where Amal fits. He's at genius level with chess, for example, similarly with jigsaws. He has amazing skills of visual memory and retention. The big problem is he's never talked."

"And can he?"

"We think so, but he's never got around to it. Maybe it will come with age. We live in hope of a miracle."

"That was quiet a detailed summary," says Tom.

"As a concerned parent, you make sure that you do the research."

Tom ruffles Amal's hair again. "So, there's a big ask there from your dad, Amal," he tells the boy. Amal continues to stare at Tom's face with the unselfconscious intensity of a baby.

I'm in danger of becoming emotional. It's a huge effort to discuss Amal rationally, like some lab specimen. "Come on, I'll show you around. Shall we start with the outside first?"

195

He drops his meagre belongings on the front steps and we amble towards the stable.

"This is Ginger, Sangita's pony. She's riding him in gymkhanas when time allows. I can see it getting less and less as 'A' levels and her violin audition approach."

Amal is stroking Ginger's head and making low level growling sounds. The pony tries to lick his face, there's clearly a bond between them.

"He loves the pony then?"

"Not as much as we'd have liked, he's keener on next door's goats. If you really want to win him over, it's plants, trees and flowers – virtually anything to do with the garden."

Tom laughs. "We should get along fine then, Amal," he says. "And Sangita's the girl that served in the shop?"

I smile. "No, that was Isha, our assistant. Sangita's seventeen and hoping to get into music college next year."

"I look forward to meeting her," he replies.

I'm growing uncomfortable. "I have to be straight with you, Tom, it's going to take some time with Jas. I'm not sure that she wants you around the kids. As I said, once she gets to know you, things will be different."

His face falls. "You said *low profile* but I didn't realise you meant *keep away.*"

"Amal's going to be following you around the garden anyway. Like I said, Jas will come around."

I take him past the tennis court to show him the allotment area and green housing. He appraises it all carefully.

"A little run-down and in need of some TLC, but all of the basics are there, Rakesh. I reckon it's been very productive in the past, the soil is excellent."

To me it looks just sad and overgrown, but what do I know? "Sounds good," I say encouragingly.

"Have you ever eaten home-grown veggies?"

"Can't say I have."

"Well there's nothing like them – no chemical fertilizers, no sprays, no poisons. They taste completely different."

I'm pleased to see his enthusiasm growing. "We can give it a try. Then there's an orchard and a big area of fruit crops. We've tasted the raspberries, very nice. That section seems to be taking care of itself."

He smiles at my ignorance. "You might think so and you'll have some kind of crop from this season, but then without proper husbandry the law of diminishing returns kicks in. It's like anything else in life, you'll get out what you put in."

"So you think we might be able to knock it all into shape?"

"Undoubtedly. You don't know what you've got here, Rakesh. It could be a little gold mine. I'd say it's been someone's small market garden in the past."

"Well, it's open house – whatever you feel you can do."

We move on towards the house.

"I'll show you the granny flat first."

We walk past the impressive front entrance, enter the annex and stand inside the little lounge. He looks really full up.

197

"It's a great thing you've done for me. At the hostel, I don't know how I'd have found the courage to get started."

I'm pleased beyond words. "I hope it's going to work out for us. I'm mobile again, it means a lot to me. Whatever else you can do is a bonus. Tomorrow, we'll take a drive over to my new supermarket."

"I presume it's that shiny monster on the drive?"

"Range Rover Super Sport – top spec'."

"Only the best for a lottery winner."

"Something like that. Anyway, I'll leave you to settle in. I'll be back in half an hour. Maybe you'll want to drive down to the nearest shops? We'll need to set you up with a few basic provisions."

I'm half way across to the main house with Amal, when it registers: *Only the best for a lottery winner.* I stagger and I'm in danger of falling. There's nothing to hold on to but Amal's hand. I told him my money was from a family inheritance – What the fuck's going on? I have to know... I *must* find a way to bring up the subject again.

Later, when I return to his front door I hear the sound of classical music from within. Sangi's made a bit of a den of the place; he must have found the hi-fi and some of her disks. No real harm in that, though I'm not sure how Jas will react if she happens to hear it?

Bloody Hell! I'm becoming totally paranoid! *I'm* the boss around here – not the woman of the family! And I've offered Tom Andrews my hospitality! If the man wants to play classical music, he can bloody well play classical music!

I ring the bell and he opens the door to me looking relaxed and smiling.

"Settled in?"

"Brilliant! I hope it's OK about the music?"

"Of course, of course. Shall we head out and get in some provisions for you?"

We walk down to the Range Rover and he spends a minute or two familiarising himself with the instruments and controls.

"More like an aircraft than a car," he comments.

"It is a bit of a beast," I say wistfully.

We take off for Bobbington.

"So, Jas is a golfer. If I'm not being too bold, when you're not at the shop, how do you spend your time?"

"I play some golf too, although, I guess some of my golfing partners would probably dispute that."

"And were you always a shopkeeper?"

"No – a postman first, the shop came later. On the Post, I was trim and healthy." I pat my belly. "The shop gave me this. Now with the inheritance, it's grown bigger again. I need to do something about it."

"So the golf's not enough?"

I laugh self-deprecatingly. "I told you, I'm crap. I've no natural talent for it. It's a rich man's game. I took it up only after the inheritance and I'm still learning."

That's twice I've edged the inheritance into the conversation. There's been no reaction. I'm beginning to think that I've read too much into his *lottery winner* comment. Maybe for him, *lottery winner* is just a synonym for *rich lucky bastard*? I feel a flood of relief.

We drive on for a while in silence, but then he returns to his mentor role. "Thinking of the trigger points: it's a real problem for you, isn't it, the money?"

Is he baiting me? Does he know something, or doesn't he? The paranoia heats up again, but doesn't exactly catch fire.

"I suppose it is, but it's probably got more to do with the relative isolation I feel out here. As I said, Sikhs are meant to grow spiritually through social interaction. I used to think that I was making a pretty good job of it back in Netherton."

"An interesting religion."

"More a way of life. We're not big on living in palaces on isolated mountain tops."

"Bobbington's hardly an isolated mountain top."

"No, but you get my drift."

"I wish I had your options. Knowing what I know now, I'd work tirelessly for my own charities."

"We've that in common," I tell him, "I intend to do more for charity, much more." I feel a glimmer of excitement, of hope, but it's far too early to risk making any further proposals about chucking money his way.

18

Life slots into a new pattern. Tom works half the day on various jobs around the property and when weather permits, the other half on the gardens. It's the gardens that show most obvious signs of improvement, he has such a talent for the work. The roses are pruned back, sprayed and fertilised, salad crops are being planted, rows of root crops are showing through in ranks of green, there are five long mounds of potato plants, the greenhouse is a mass of green young seedlings, the lawns have been scarified – it's a term he had to explain to me – and the orchards sprayed and fitted with new irrigation pipes.

As for Tom, he looks fitter and younger by the day. He's tidied himself up. I've bought him work clothes and I've accompanied him to purchase a new wardrobe. We've visited the barber (though not for me, of course) and he's taken to using deodorant – I can smell it when I enter the annex. He scrubs up well.

I let Amal follow him around when Jas is out of the way and have got to thinking that maybe one day, my son could become a gardener of sorts? I hadn't intended to become quite so tied up with it all, but Tom is forever in need of equipment, tools and materials. We have a daily council of war and more often than not, Amal and I end up accompanying him to some supplier or other. The first time that we entered our neighbouring garden centre – a Sikh, a wasted-looking scruffy guy and a special needs kid – they seemed a little sniffy. Over the weeks, with their till playing *The Sound of Music* with my fifty pound notes, they've drastically revised their attitude.

Twice a week I'm back to my golf. It took a letter of apology to the club captain and one to Dave, my new engineering friend. He's a decent bloke and we hack our way around together. We have a laugh now about our first meeting. Tom also drops me off at the driving range for a couple of hours on a Thursday morning. I've improved a little. My other partner is a dentist called Stan Field; I met him at the driving range and we hit it off (excuse the pun). If anything, I'm slightly better than him. I certainly hope that he pulls teeth better than he hits a ball down the fairway. Jas wouldn't be seen dead playing with any of us.

Lately, my visits to the shop have not been much more than token appearances. I've come to accept that they're far better off without me. I'm sure they got news of my crash and driving ban, after all, it was all over the local freebie newspaper. Isha must find it strange to see the drunk she knew at the former shop chauffeuring me around. They make no comment, I pay them, they turn in a handsome profit. The ban was for three years and it came with a five hundred pound fine. The worst part was the humiliating court appearance before a middle-aged, county lady. I was made to feel like a common criminal, though I can't say I didn't deserve it.

Jas has said very little about the new arrangement. She'd rather die than admit it, but I think she's secretly pleased. She gets her car hand-washed by Tom twice a week and she loves the improvements to the property and grounds. She affects to studiously ignore his efforts, but I catch her out in the gardens, walking around examining things minutely. She hasn't been able to resist asking when the first of the fresh produce will be ready for the table and she's suggested items to me that we might grow. She knows too that her worst fears haven't been realised: Tom hasn't dragged me down into an orgy of day-time drinking – quite the reverse, it's obvious he's helped keep me dry.

I dream one night of Balkar. We're in New Delhi. He's a beggar on the pavement. He has an enormous green head and red staring eyes. He's sitting next to a weighing machine and the big hand on it is pointing to two hundred thousand pounds. In his hands he's holding two large begging cups. I walk around him, intending to ignore his supplications but his arms extend, longer and longer until they become two serpents that rise and coil around my neck. I awaken, choking and trembling and Jas is already sitting up in bed staring at me.

"Are you OK?" she enquires.

"Fine, fine. Just a stupid, horrible dream. God, for a minute, Jas, it was like returning to the heebie-jeebies I was getting from the alcohol."

I lie back and allow my breathing to slow down. She snuggles in close.

"I'm fine now," I tell her eventually.

"Make love to me, Rakki."

We've done it a few times since my recovery, but this is new, it's been years since she took the initiative. An olive branch. I resist the temptation to mention that we've got a lot to thank Tom for – that would be a real passion-killer! We begin slowly and tenderly and end in a frenzy of resurgent desire. It's as good as it's ever been. By the time we're spent, the dawn is flooding through our window. I stretch and offer to make tea.

She traces a finger around my belly-button. "You need to do something about this tummy," she observes.

"Vorsprung durch Tecknik," I say.

"What does that mean?"

"I dunno, it's about a German car – comfortable and bouncy – I might be wrong."

"So, how long d'you reckon he'll be staying?" she asks, neutrally.

"It's open-ended. You're happy enough with the way it's going, aren't you?"

"It can't be forever, Rakki. You've a full three years to manage without the car."

"I know that, Love. He's a very talented guy, he'll be wanting to move on soon enough."

"And when he does, you'll get yourself a driver?"

"I suppose so."

"I'd feel happier. We'd need a gardener too."

"But why push it, Jas? You've got your mates and the golf. I'm pleased to have wheels again and look at the general improvements. Surely things can stay that way for a while longer?"

She shrugs, but there's none of the old hostility there. It's the nearest that Jas will ever get to admitting that there are positives in the arrangement.

I move to get up.

"Don't bother," she says. "I'll make tea. I need to get a move on, there's a committee meeting at the club this morning. What are your plans?"

"You know I told you about the dentist guy? He's buying me lunch at the club, then we're playing eighteen holes later."

"Not a liquid one, I trust?"

"Jas!" I respond. She's half-joking, but deep down I know she's still half-serious.

I lie back and remember the dream. It's a stark reminder that apart from putting the money in place, I've done bugger-all about Balkar. I've had no desire to be the one to make the first move. Dumb strategy, I don't want the bastard turning up here with an ultimatum. Jas drops me off a cuppa. She tells me she'll be back early afternoon, then disappears into the bathroom. I resolve to ring him today. I'll do it from my clubhouse, after the game.

19

I beat Stan by five strokes; we finish an hour early and I'm feeling bullish. I'm the only one drinking slim-line tonic with a slice at the club bar, but that feels pretty good too: empowering. Two of my early less-than-enthusiastic partners, Malcolm and Tim, followed us around the course and they've just walked into the bar. They're friendly enough now that there's no chance of me going out with them again. Malcolm offers me a drink and I politely refuse. He's maybe twenty years older than me and a fellow whisky *aficionado*. His eyes are beginning to yellow and the small capillaries on the surface of his cheeks and nose give him the appearance of having just stepped off an Icelandic fishing boat. Unless he gets himself to AA, he's for an early grave. It's perverse to feel smug about something like that, but I do.

I swap pleasantries with a couple of other members. I'm relaxed in spite of the call I know I have to make. It's almost five, Tom's not due to collect me for another hour. Still plenty of time for Balkar. My mobile rings, I look at the name on screen and curse myself for tempting fate! I feel my heart misbeat a couple of times as I cross to a quieter corner of the bar. Bloody ticker – it's done that a few times lately.

"Hi, Balkar, I was about to ring you." I try for enthusiasm but sound as though I'm responding to the tax collector. In a way, I am.

"Is that my fellow millionaire?"

"*Fellow* millionaire?"

"That's right, man, the price has just gone up. I want half."

"Tell me you're taking the piss!"

"I'm deadly serious, Rakki. You're a lazy, uncaring bastard and I've heard nothing from you."

"Look, if that's all that's worrying you, the money's–"

"I've already been spending on account."

"I've *got* it, that's what I'm telling you! It's waiting."

"You're not listening, man, I said I want *half*."

"You know that's impossible."

"I met up with a little guy called Tom. It was a bit of a game changer. What d'you call him, by the way? Tom the handyman? Tom the gardener? Tom the chauffeur? Or: Tom-the-poor-bastard-who-if-there-was-any-fairness-in-this-world-should-be-bathing-in-goat's-milk?"

"Who … how …?" I'm dumbstruck, gasping for air. Whatever my heart was doing before, it's now threatening to burst my chest.

"You've re-homed him. What a pathetic, bleeding-hearts conscience you must have! Anyway, as I was saying, the price is now half, otherwise I'm betting on a little friendly negotiation with Tom before I take him down to sign depositions at your local cop shop."

"You've told him?"

"Get real! You're my most reliable partner. I'm just talking strategic responses of final resort. Besides, you and I are mates, it won't have to come to that. I want a fairer cut, that's all."

"Half is ridiculous! I'd have to sell up."

"Take a loan against the property, the profits from your new supermarket and interest on the rest of your pile would pay off the instalments. You're rolling in it, my friend. I don't give a damn how you do it – just do it!

"How the hell did you know about the supermarket?"

"I read the papers, keep my nose to the ground."

"I can't see -"

"You're out of options, mate."

"I could tell him myself, then have the police on you for blackmail – we'd go down together."

He chuckles. "*You'd* go down, Rakesh. All I've had out of this is a pint of bitter at Ma Pardoe's. I'm clean as a whistle and my patience is really wearing thin now."

"You bastard!"

"You've got a month, otherwise Tom and I are going to have that conversation."

The screen disappears. I hit re-call. He ignores it. I try three times, same result. I walk through to the Gents' toilet and splash water on my face. I know I'm going to have to get a heart check before long, the missed beats are back. I'm shaking all over.

He's been to the house! It must have been today. Did he speak with Tom? Oh my God, maybe he's spoken with Jas? Do I ring Tom, get him to fetch me early? The room's beginning to spin. I'm full of unanswered questions. I'm in danger of passing out.

I return to the bar. I have to compose myself, get a grip, do some straight thinking. How in hell am I going to make small talk with Tom on the way home? It's no good, tonic water's not going to do it.

"Give me a double whisky, Dean."

"I thought you were on the wagon, Mr Basra?"

"Are you my bloody keeper, now?"

"Sorry, no offence."

He hastens to fetch me a large glass and he's away long enough for me to reflect on all that I'm throwing away. He places the drink on the bar before me. I reach for it and down it in one. I hardly feel it even touching the sides. Oh God, I'd forgotten just how good that feels! I demand a refill and this time he responds without hesitation.

I savour the second one, but for only slightly longer. I could put my mouth to the bung of a vat-full and drink myself to *oblivion.* They talk of music calming the savage breast: it's whisky every time! However did those dark, hairy little buggers from north of the Border ever hit upon the recipe? It must have been divine intervention, compensation for all of the shit weather they get. I sit on a high bar stool swallowing refills. I'm getting a few disapproving looks, maybe one or two of the members remember my last binge. *Fuck 'em.*

I've had a fair few but I'm still clear-headed. Through the large mirror behind the bar I see Tom entering the club lounge. He spots me on the bar stool and his face drops.

"Rakesh! What in hell are you *doing?*"

Who on earth does he think he's talking to? He's no more than an *employee* of mine! I manage to transfer my anger and point at Dean. "I've fucking told *him* already, it's no-one else's business, but mine!"

"Language, please, Mr Basra," says Dean. "Remember the membership rules."

It takes a supreme effort for me not to leap over the bar and punch out his lights. Tom holds on to my shoulders. Even through the gathering fog, I realise that this is way out of character. I'm always the original Mr Nice Guy after a few drinks, at peace with the entire world.

"Come on Rakesh," says Tom, gently, "this is getting us nowhere."

I'm suddenly grateful for his care. Guilty as sin over my behaviour and the anger, aggression and negativity. I could burst into tears. I'm totally fucking lost. He half lifts me from the stool and begins to propel me towards the exit. I offer no resistance. The cooler air outside does me good and my head clears sufficiently to speak coherently.

"I'm sorry, mate. Making a bloody fool of myself. Good job you came."

He reaches into the Range Rover for a flask. "Here, have some of this, it's black coffee. Lucky I put it in the wagon."

It's still scalding hot. I lean against the car and sip it slowly. The caffeine begins to win back a few brain cells.

"Let's go," suggests Tom.

We've climbed into the car. I'm still sipping coffee and my brain is back in its box, racing around and banging against the sides, but it's not geared for subtlety.

"Did someone call at the house?"

He seems to ignore the question. "That's such a bitch, Rakesh, and you've been doing so well."

"No matter."

"You have to see it as just a one off and start all over. It's so -"

"Did you hear what I asked you?"

"Yeah. I thought about coming earlier, but then thought better of it."

"Why?"

"Well – your wife seemed pretty upset."

"So there *was* somebody?"

He remains silent. The whisky is making me irritable again.

"Tom, for fuck's sake?"

"Maybe it was her brother, your brother – it's no business of mine, but I think maybe you've got trouble in the family."

"Can you spell it out then, what happened?"

"He was an Asian guy with a shiny new black BMW. Seemed very pleasant, chatted with me for a while and then went into the house. There was some shouting when he left and as I say, Jasvinder seemed upset."

I remember Balkar's ambition to own a black Beamer. "What did he look like?"

"Like an all-in wrestler, with a shaven head and a ring in his right ear."

Balkar for certain. I try to keep the tremor from my voice.

"It's not family trouble. He's a friend of mine called Balkar. So, what did he have to say?"

"Pleasantries, that's all. Asked me who I was, how long I'd been working for you, stuff like that. One thing was weird – he called me 'The famous Tom'. I guess you must have mentioned me?"

"Probably did, come to think of it. But you've no idea what's upset Jas?"

"I was sitting on board the mower most of the time. When I did switch off I could hear her voice raised and coming from inside the house. She sounded so upset, I was at the point of going and asking if everything was all right, to be honest, but then they came out. Your wife stood at the door shouting after him in Punjabi, I couldn't understand a thing, of course. He didn't seem anywhere near as disturbed as she was. Then he drove off like a maniac."

He's told her *everything!* God Almighty.

I'm shaking again. I take a deep breath. "You've got to give me a minute, I need to make a call."

I open the car door and begin to climb out.

"Christ! I hope I've done the right thing in telling you?" he says, looking upset.

"You have, you have."

I slam the door shut and stride over to some bushes near the first tee. My mobile's already in my hand and I speed-dial her number. The thumping sound in my ears is so loud I fear I might not hear her. There's no reply. *Fuck!* What's happening? I dial the house number and it rings through to our answer-message.

"Jas, if you're there, give me a ring right now."

I wait a few moments, cursing myself for not having dealt with Balkar when things were still manageable. There's still no reply. I return to the car and say nothing. Tom is looking anxious, but that's the least of my problems. He starts for home. God knows how I'm going to face her, or what in hell I'm going to say to her.

"I'm really gutted about your drinking, Rakesh," says Tom.

"*Fuck* the drinking!" I tell him savagely. It shuts him up and we drive the rest of the way in silence. He's a true friend and deserves better, but I can't bring myself to open conversation again.

I turn the key and walk in. I'm relieved to find her home. She's sitting on one of the wide settees in the big, open-plan lounge. She comes towards me and I think she's going to attack me. I've never seen her in such a state. I get in first.

"Jas, I know he's been here. I'm so damned sorry that it had to come out like that."

"You tell me *everything* right now, chapter and verse, you cheating swine! Then I'm walking, Rakesh. It's over between us!"

It's as though I've been punched full on the jaw. I expected anger, tears, bitter disappointment, fear of my imminent arrest even …

"Jas! I beg you! I can't tell you how many times I've tried, how many times I've been on the point of confessing."

She collapses onto a settee, wracked by long, painful sobs. "How could you be such a snivelling coward? *Everybody* must know! It takes your bloody mate to come and try it on with me, before your wife finds out!"

I'm deeply confused now. "Try it on with you? What the hell are you talking about?"

"*Balkar* – you fool! One minute I'm making him an orange juice at the kitchen sink, the next minute he's got his paws all over me, trying to kiss me."

"What! – I'll kill him! How? Why? What did he tell you?"

Time passes before she can control the sobbing enough to be coherent. "He's telling me about his big new BMW and all the money that's coming his way, then he makes a pass, tries to kiss me and asks me to go away with him."

"I'll swing for him, I swear it! I should have been here to protect you."

"But you chose to be with *her* – is that it? Don't you come anywhere near me! That's what money brings is it? Drinking yourself stupid and then finding another woman!"

I'm thunderstruck. I'm beyond *thunderstruck.* I can't believe my ears. "Woman! What in hell has he been telling you?" I shout.

"He didn't have to tell me *anything!* The insinuations couldn't have been more obvious!"

"What insinuations, for God's sake?"

"I slapped his face to stop him and out it came: *'You don't know, do you? Poor Jasvinder. If only you knew the half of it!'* His exact words! What don't I know the half of? What else could it bloody mean? You're having an affair! Why else would he have dreamed he could come on to me – his friend's wife? I'm fair game because I'm poor Jasvinder, the wife who's been cast aside, the cheated partner! At least show me enough respect now to be honest, Rakesh. At least be man enough to come clean with it."

She puts her head in her hands and the sound she makes is a low-pitched guttural howling, like something I've never heard before and hope never to hear again. I go over to her and place an arm around her and I'm grateful that she doesn't push me away. Her entire body is shaken by the sobbing and I can only wait awhile for it to subside.

20

I'm not sure where to start. I could never have imagined at the beginning of the afternoon that actually, I'd be pleased to tell her the truth, pleased and relieved.

"D'you know where his black BMW comes from?"

"He's making money. What's that got to do with anything?" she answers sullenly. She's stopped crying, although there are small after-shocks like the aftermath of an earthquake.

"Not *making* money – no Jas – he's after *our* money! That's what this is now about."

"*Our* money? He's after *our* money?"

"Not even ours, really – the money's all his. Tom's. Him out there in the granny annex."

She understands nothing and the anger begins to rise. "You're making no sense at all! I'm talking about *us* – you – you and your bloody affair!"

"Jas, *listen!* Remember the Sunday morning when you chucked Tom out? Remember what I was doing? I was checking his lottery ticket – the *winning* ticket."

It's so far from her current state of mind that it takes a moment or two to sink in. Her eyes have grown large and round, like a child's in mid-story, at bedtime.

"It can't be true. It was *days* after when you checked your ticket and found out – it was the *Wednesday morning!*"

"I kept the ticket on a shelf, Jas. That first day, it was genuinely just the circumstances; then I'm ashamed to say, he didn't come back and I didn't go looking for him. I made the mistake of discussing what to do with Balkar at the pub. Remember, the Tuesday night out, the 'business meeting' I had with him? Well, now he's turned to blackmail. But rightfully, it's all his, *everything* – it all belongs to Tom Andrews."

She is stupefied. I couldn't have shocked her more if I'd have suddenly grown a second head. There's a trace of relief there too, relief that her husband is a common thief rather than an adulterer. *Poor Jas.*

"I can't take it in!"

She's deathly pale, pressing the fingers of both hands so deeply into her cheeks that they're beginning to whiten at the knuckle.

"It's true Jas, all of it. I'm so sorry."

"But, but – how – Does he know?"

"Tom? No, of course he doesn't."

"But Rakesh – you know we have to tell him?"

I nod my silent agreement.

"And that's why -"

"And that's why Balkar came around here and tried it on. He must have lost the plot entirely. Bastard! He's always believed that he was God's gift to women. Originally, he demanded two hundred thousand to keep quiet about the win."

"And you paid him?"

"No, that's the problem. He must have been spending in anticipation. He's so full of himself."

"Before he made a grab at me he asked me if I'd fancy him if he was rich."

"There you are then – he always joked you chose the wrong man. Bastard! It must have been right after you kicked him out that he rang me. It put the price up."

"Oh my God! Oh my God!

It's fully hit her now and she's on her feet, gasping in disbelief, pacing the floor. She begins to hyperventilate and I sit her back down and cross to the kitchen for water. She drinks and puts her head in her hands. I'm no longer sure what to expect.

"You'll give him nothing, Rakesh, *nothing!*"

"Of course not. I know that now. I'm so sorry for everything, Jas, I truly am."

We're on our feet facing each other and suddenly she's in my arms, clinging to me for grim death.

"Oh my poor, stupid Rakesh!"

I stroke the back of her head. "How could you ever have believed that there was somebody else?"

She's sobbing into my shoulder. "My world fell apart. I couldn't think of any other possible meaning to his words."

We're quiet for a few minutes, just enjoying the warmth of each other's proximity and inwardly celebrating our renewed love for each other. Finally we break and sit together on the nearest settee. We face each other, holding hands.

"So what now? I ask.

"There's no argument, we have to give it back to him, every single penny."

It was what I was expecting and I'm glad of it. It's as though a huge weight has lifted from me. "I agree. It won't be easy, Jas, he may press charges – even demand lost interest on his capital. I could go to prison."

"I don't care *what* it takes. I want my husband back, the man I married."

I'm overwhelmed. Humbled by her nobility, emotionally in pieces. The tears flow like fountains. In my shame, I put my head in her lap. "I did – I did – I did it for you and Sangi and, and – Amal," I choke.

"Oh, my Rakesh, my poor, poor, misguided Rakki ..." she croons.

We doze a little. The strain of the past few hours have been immense. Jas stirs and I awaken. She rises and offers to make herb tea. We sit side by side, lost in thought, sipping the reviving liquid.

"It means saying goodbye to all of this."

She shrugs, dismissively.

"Maybe, he'd allow me to hold on to the supermarket? If we can just find somewhere to stay. It's making good money, I could pay him anything outstanding from part of the income?"

She shakes her head. "Too early for any of that, Rakesh. As you said, we don't know what his reaction will be. The first step is to tell him."

"I'd like to get that over and done with."

"Agreed. Then there's no time like the present."

We finish our drinks and I glance at my watch. "It's seven thirty, he may be eating." One glance at her and I add, "But let's give it a try."

We put on outdoor jackets, pass through the front door and walk over to the granny flat. The blinds are drawn but there's light showing behind them. I ignore the bell, knock firmly, my heart in my mouth. He opens the door a chink and registers surprise and not a little concern.

"Sorry to bother you, Tom," I begin, "but may we come in and have a word with you?"

His concern seems to deepen to alarm. "It's not that convenient, right now," he stutters.

We've got this far and there's no turning back. Jas looks equally determined.

"Tom, I know I haven't been the most welcoming of people and for that I apologise," she says. "But if you don't mind, we have something really important to say and it just won't wait." She takes another step forward and Tom takes an involuntary step back. The door swings inward and reveals our daughter standing there behind him, looking scared out of her wits.

"What on earth …?" Jas manages. She pushes past Tom into the room and I follow.

"What are you doing in here?" Jas demands.

"Mum, Mum – I can explain!" cries Sangita.

I can't suppress recent memories, the horrendous upset over Sangi and her young boyfriend – even though my head tells me that any comparison is ridiculous.

"Rakesh, let me -" begins Tom, but Jas has lost it completely.

"Didn't I tell you to stay away from this man!" she shouts, grabbing our daughter by the shoulders.

"Mum! Mum! Will you listen!" cries Sangita.

Tom takes a step towards Jas, but she pushes him aside. She too must have recent memories at the forefront of her mind and they're mixing toxically with her earlier opposition to him. She propels Sangi forward, ready to listen to no one.

"Get out of here right now!" she demands.

"Mummy, I hate you!" shouts Sangi. "He's a lovely, kind man – *nothing* like you've said! He's been helping me with my music!"

She wrenches herself free from her mother and dives past us out into the garden.

"Sangi! Sangi!" I shout and chase out after her. She has a head start across the grounds towards the stable. Another thought flashes to the forefront of my mind: if Sangita was in there with Tom, *where the devil is Amal?* I stop in my tracks, turn and run back towards the flat. Jas is coming out through the door.

"Where's Amal?" I yell.

It dawns on Jas and she looks panic stricken. With all of the heavy emotional drama, neither of us have given him a thought.

"I thought he was with Sangita!" she shouts.

"Amal! Amal!" I scream. "Amal!"

I run towards the tennis court and check myself again. Where is he most likely to be? In the house maybe? Did we leave the swimming pool locked or open? God knows! I have this terrible vision of him lying motionless at the bottom of the pool. Fucking filthy pool! I'm going to fill it in, replace it with a badminton court.

I turn in mid-stride again, start running towards the house and suddenly, I feel as though I've been kicked in the chest by a horse. The pain is horrible, it's extending up my neck and down my right arm. I stagger and fall. There's a moment of blackness and then things swim back into view. I'm flat on my back in the drive close by the steps to the main door. I must have been out for a second or two. Jas and Tom are looking down anxiously into my face. The pain is unbearable, I feel as though I'm being crushed by a large rock.

"Are you all right? Are you all right, Rakki?" Jas is repeating.

"The pain – my chest, my jaw…" I manage.

"I think it's a heart attack!" I hear Tom tell her. "You call for an ambulance! I'll get him in the recovery position." He pulls me onto my side and puts me into a foetal position. "Good. Can you hear me, Rakesh? Try to breath and keep calm. We'll get a blanket under you. You just hang on in now, we're going to get some help."

I lie fighting the pain, trying to breathe, worrying about my son. Jas is next to me, holding my hand. Sangi's tearful face appears above me – and Amal too, thank God.

"I'm so sorry, Dad," Sangi cries. "I didn't know you were looking for Amal – he was with me, reading a gardening book in Tom's kitchen."

I think I hear a siren in the distance.

21

It's been five days, they're discharging me this afternoon.
I've been very lucky. I was rushed straight to Sandwell
General Hospital's dedicated Heart Attack Centre. They
tell me that as heart attacks go, it was relatively mild. It
certainly didn't feel that way. I'm going to be on ACE
Inhibitors and Statins from now on – the first looks after
the blood pressure and the second sorts out the cholesterol
level; they were both in a parlous state. I'm being referred
to the Cardiac Rehabilitation Service. There's a fully
equipped gym there and they run a pretty rigorous training
programme. I've been told that patients who were in a far
worse state than me have gone on to compete in the
London Marathon! All in all, it's a bloody amazing
service they run. When you don't need these people, you
never think about them. It's like the fire fighters and the
ambulance crews – thank God they're there in the
background for us all.

I can't drive for a month and I hadn't the heart to tell
them I'm banned. We're supposed to reintroduce sex very
carefully – but I'm saying nothing about my erectile
dysfunction, either. They've also spent time with me
looking at my risk factors: life style, body-fat index, diet
and stress. I'm fine about tackling the weight, the diet and
the exercise, but I can hardly come clean about the stress

factors affecting my life. I lied about the alcohol too. I wrote: 'reformed alcoholic'. Jas thinks that was stupid given my recent sudden relapse, but this time I'm going to climb back on the wagon and I know I'll stay there. Finally, I got a gold star for being a non-smoker.

Jas has been wonderful, in spite of what lies ahead and how it must be weighing on her mind. There was more than enough to worry about when we knocked on Tom's front door and now there's been all of this. For the first day or two, all of her care and attention was upon me, then when I was out of imminent danger, her thoughts began to turn to the other issues. When we discuss the end of our current lifestyle and approaches to an unknown future she's so matter of fact. Last night she told me that it will be worth a thousand lottery wins to close our eyes with a wholesome conscience and to fall into innocent sleep. It humbled me and made me feel that some good can come out of the worst of situations. We're closer than ever before, but we're under no illusions – Balkar is still out there and we have yet to tell Tom and to deal with the aftermath.

We're sitting on the bed, waiting for my consultant to come and give the all clear for my release. Jas tells me that she's been dealing with a few issues of her own. She's made her peace with Tom and although I'd never dream of saying it, maybe a little humble pie has been a good thing for her.

"Did you know he's a very accomplished pianist?" she asks.

"No idea."

"He wanted to attend the RCM himself, but his father pushed him into accountancy."

"You *have* been having a heart to heart."

She reddens slightly. "He tried to apologise over seeing Sangi behind our backs. She's such a little minx! Apparently, she was so fearful about all of the Saturday practices she'd skipped that he began to advise her on interpretation of the audition pieces."

"So, that's the explanation."

"And you really knew nothing?"

"About what you've just told me – not a darned thing, Jas."

She nods in acknowledgement. "But you did know that Amal follows him around the garden like a puppy?"

I nod guiltily. "I couldn't see any harm in it. Amal's plant crazy, it would have been impossible to keep him away."

She smiles. "You were right – he's good and kind and Amal seems to love him."

My face falls. "It's going to be such a wrench for the kids."

"You're well enough to know: there's an added urgency, he's planning on leaving quite soon."

"Because of the embarrassment over Sangi?"

"No, I've told you – he's apologised, I've apologised. He's been very gracious. He told me that being with us has given him the boost he needed. He wants to rent a flat in Stourbridge and take on some accountancy work. He's very positive, talking about part-time teaching of the piano and maybe even a return to property development."

"Let's hope he feels the same way about everything when he knows the whole story."

We fall silent, weighed down by the task ahead.

"He's very upset that you've started to drink again."

I'm so ashamed that I can hardly look her in the eyes. It seems almost a bigger betrayal than keeping quiet about the lottery ticket.

"You know the background now, the pressure I was under. But something's lifted, Jas. Telling you has changed everything."

"And you're sure about that?"

"Sure and certain. I've had this scare too. I'm not going to let the whisky put me in a wooden box." She looks a little more reassured. "Telling Tom will complete the cure. I'll keep up the connection with AA, in Dudley, though. I'm just hoping that he'll want to remain on speaking terms."

My specialist bustles in, trailed by a couple of student doctors. The man is *God.* I think so and judging by their expressions, so do the student doctors. Jas gets up, as if to leave.

"You're fine where you are, Mrs Basra," he tells her. He's studying my notes intently. "I think we're all done for now," he says with a smile. "You've had all of the debriefings, I take it?"

"Yes, Mr Simms," I reply.

"Good, good, good." He reaches for my pulse, almost as an afterthought. "Excellent. Yes. Well – follow everything to the letter and I think we've got an excellent chance of rearing you."

He does a fair bit of scribbling on some forms and passes me one to sign.

"You're free to go. Pop along to the desk on the way out and they'll sort out your medication and the first of your out-patient appointments."

I try to thank him but he holds up a hand to cut me short. "Just take care of yourself. Our thanks lie in seeing people walk out of here."

Jas leads us down the long corridors towards Reception. She's carrying my small overnight case; I feel like a cripple.

"He's waiting in your car."

"Oh, right. You didn't tell me?"

"I asked him to come. There's more leg room in yours and it seemed the right thing to do."

"That's thoughtful." I stop in the middle of the corridor. "Jas, I'm going to tell him on the way home."

"The sooner the better. It's on both of our consciences now."

We cross the car park. The driver's window is open and I can see that Tom has dozed off. I tap him gently on the shoulder and smile broadly as he opens his eyes.

"Ah, sorry about that. Listening to some Brahms, it always has that effect upon me."

I've never heard of Brahms and don't like to ask. That's another 'new life' resolution: to learn more about classical music. Maybe a 'near death' experience has that effect upon you? You're crammed full with new resolutions.

Tom slings my suitcase in the boot and attempts to apologise over Sangi. I'm quick to tell him that Jas has explained everything.

"I've been beating myself up that it was the cause of the heart attack," he says.

"Nothing to do with it, Tom, believe me. They tell me that I've been a sure-fire candidate for some time. Besides, I've got much bigger things on my mind to talk about." I reply.

Jas and I climb in together onto the broad back seat.

"So how are you feeling now?" he asks, as we pull away.

"Fitter than a butcher's dog!"

"Whoa, whoa!" says Jas. "I don't think he'll be chasing after bones for some time yet."

That makes Tom laugh.

"Seriously though," I say, "they're bloody marvellous in there. I'm going to start raising money for them."

Jas gives me a quick, sharp look.

"Well, I guess you can afford the odd quid or two," says Tom.

We drive on in silence. I'm trying to find the courage, trying to find the words. Now, I've left it almost too late, we're about half a mile from home. Jas gives me a painful nudge in the ribs and mouths the words: "Go on!"

"You're leaving soon then, Tom?"

"Tomorrow."

"*Tomorrow!*" we say in unison.

He half-turns in the driving seat before looking back to the road. "I'm sorry to drop it on you like this. The agent's found me a flat with vacant possession – there's been half a dozen other people chasing it – he's done me a favour but it meant an immediate decision. Don't worry, I'm still planning on coming over to help you out."

228

"We have to talk money, Tom, there's something you *have* to know."

"I know already."

Jas and I move forward on our seat.

"It's the massive fortune you owe me."

"You *know* about it?"

He chuckles. "You told me when I moved in – you'd be putting my wages aside. I *do* need them now, I have to admit. I hope it won't break the bank? I have to find the deposit and the first month's rent."

"It's more than that, Tom. I've done you a terrible wrong."

"In giving me a half-way house? A job? A purpose? Some self-respect? In sharing your wonderful family with me?"

"No. Listen!"

"I've told Jas – make no mistake, Rakesh – it's your kindness and hospitality and getting to know your kids, that's got me over the hump. I want to go out there now and try to make a difference in the world."

"Listen, will you! It goes back to that last time you came in the shop when you were having the argument with Jas and I -"

"Water under the bridge. As I told you: that part of my life is history. I don't want you dwelling on it."

We're passing through our gates and Sangi and Amal are waiting at the end of the drive for us. I can see Tom's gaze upon me in the driving mirror, but I can't read him. Jas pokes me again.

"I can't leave it like this, Tom. We need to talk again."

He fails to reply, already, he's hooting the horn and smiling and waving at the children.

22

We eat. Jas sees Amal to bed and Sangi goes off for a swim.

"You have to try again, Rakki," Jas tells me.

"I know. It's like he doesn't want to hear. D'you think he does know something?"

"Do *you*? You're better placed to judge than me?"

"The first thing I did when we met was to offer him money, you know."

"And did he take any?"

"Refused outright. He told me he'd been a gambler before becoming a drunk. That's why he wanted me to hold his wages for him – worried that cash would set him off gambling again."

"It didn't stop him from doing the Lottery, did it?"

"True. It must have been a token, his way of affirming that he had the gambling under control? With the Lottery you don't chase lost money with new bets, like you do with horses, or gaming machines. For him the drink was only incidental."

"Poor Tom, think what it cost him. Afterwards… d'you think there's a chance he might get back with his wife?"

I shake my head. "It's a sad tale. After the divorce, she married his younger brother. She'd turned to him for help when Tom was at his worst and they ended up together. According to Tom, it might have been going on earlier; he worked long hours developing the properties that he purchased."

"Oh, the poor man. And there were no children?"

I shake my head. "She never wanted them – now she's had two with the brother. That must be so hard. I reckon it's why he's so keen on Sangi and Amal."

"So, *does* he guess something, or know something, or doesn't he?"

"I can't see how it's possible. Anyway, it changes nothing. The money's *his* – his to burn, his to paper the walls with, his to give away."

"Agreed. I just hope that it doesn't push him back into his old ways."

"Me too."

I'm overcome with fatigue. The past few days have been traumatic and I have to remember that I'm only at an early stage of recovery.

"I'm pretty tired now, Jas. I know it's not even nine, but I think I'll have my tablets and call it a day."

"And you'll try again tomorrow?"

"I'll try again tomorrow."

I'm out the minute my head hits the pillow. I'm aware of nothing, not Jas spending her customary fifteen minutes in the en-suite, nor her entering the bed. The first thing I know is she's fully dressed and gently shaking me. The sun is shining through the curtains, it's a new day already. I feel drugged, full of sleep.

"Rakki, it's nine-thirty. I wanted to let you sleep longer, but Tom came around to say his taxi will be here in an hour."

"*Shit!* So early? I'll get dressed."

I dress without a shower. I'm still feeling pretty shaky. I guess the new drug regime will take a bit of getting used to... or maybe it's the thought of what's to come with Tom.

Breakfast is on the table. It's muesli and an apple. I *hate* muesli – you might as well eat sawdust, road grit and honey – but Jas has the hospital diet sheet out on the kitchen table and she has what I call her 'lion-tamer' look about her. It seems I can say goodbye to thick-buttered toast and eggs, sunny-side up. She's reading the bloody thing as though it's a religious scroll.

It's a beautiful morning. The kids have been told not to bother Tom whilst he packs, though from what I remember, he could get all of his stuff into one red-spotted handkerchief. They're down at the stable. Sangi will be mucking out Ginger and Amal will be mucking about. (I'm pleased with that one as the puns haven't been coming so regularly lately.) I struggle with the muesli. Jas thinks I should go directly to the annex to speak to him before we all get tangled into goodbyes. I know she's right but I feel chivvied and resentful – it's not as though we're never going to see him again.

Too much information. My head's buzzing and I'm feeling weak. I tell her first I have to go and make urgent use of the toilet. I'm unsure whether it's a side-effect of the pill regime or the new salady/fruity/vegetably rabbit-food diet? Jas is patient, she knows I've been through a fair bit. Now she tells me to take my time. She doesn't want to see me keeling over. Life's complicated. I head for the little room. I'm feeling so fucking *nervous.*

Finally I'm ready. We make for the front door. I can see it's already too late for the man-to-man meeting in his flat. He's in the garden and his rucksack is sitting on the drive. He's taking a tour of the flower beds, holding hands with Amal. Sangi must still be with her pony. We make our way over. To my amazement I'm sure I hear Amal *say* something. It sounded like a foreign language. He's looking at Tom and pointing at a flower.

Jas has picked up on it too. "He's talking!" she cries.

Tom smiles a greeting. He turns towards my son. "Well, we do have the odd conversation together, don't we, Amal?"

Amal is pointing at another flower. "*Saintpaulia ionantha,*" he's saying and looking to Tom for confirmation.

"That's right, mate – it's a species of African Violet."

Jas and I stand, mesmerised, as Amal points to a big, long, colourful flower.

"*Kniphofia.*" says Amal.

Tom nods.

"*Asphodeloideae* from *Xanthorrhoeaceae,*" says Amal.

"But remember it's common name: *Red Hot Poker,*" says Tom. He turns to us. "*Kniphofia's* the botanical name of the Red Hot Poker; then Amal was giving us the sub-group and the genus."

I haven't the faintest idea what he's on about, but Amal is *talking!*

"Amal! Amal! You're talking!" I shout.

Jas and I grab hold of each other and do a little jig. I've never been so excited in my life. I grab the poor lad in a bear hug and lift him off his feet together with his mum.

"Your heart, Rakki!" shrieks Jas.

I put them down. Her focus is really much more on Amal than on my ticker, but that's absolutely *fine!*

"He knows several hundred like that," says Tom, "but all in Latin."

"It's a miracle," cries Jas and to everyone's surprise she grabs Tom around the neck and plants a big kiss on his cheek.

"Remember the plant encyclopaedia we bought at the garden centre? Amal picked it up one day and I've been pointing out things to him ever since," Tom tells us. "He's got the Latin – now all you have to do now is teach him English and Punjabi!"

Amal smiles.

"He's responding too," I say. "I can't believe it."

"It's what I've always prayed for," exclaims Jas. The tears are flowing down her face. We can't help ourselves, we do another little jig on the path.

Tom looks mildly embarrassed and not a little proud. "Hope you don't mind, I've given him the encyclopaedia. I've left it for him in the annex."

Sangi is walking up the drive towards us. Her big brown eyes are open wide. I'm sure she thinks that we've all gone stark, raving mad. We tell her the good news and she joins us in yet another little jig.

"Well – I guess this is it for a while," says Tom. "The taxi's on its way. If I could just trouble you for that money, Rakesh?"

Jas flashes me one of her strong meaningful looks and shuttles the children back down the path. "Your dad's got some very important business to discuss," she tells them.

I invite Tom back to the house. I've grown so tense, he must be able to read on my face that I've got more on my mind than simply his wages. He nods but his expression remains neutral.

When we're half way towards the front steps a car turns in through the gates at the end of the driveway. At first I think it's his taxi, but no – it's Balkar's shiny, new Beamer! I feel as though we've all entered a time warp, a state of suspended animation wherein the only moving object in the universe is Balkar's car making its way up the drive. He pulls up before us and the moment breaks. I grip Tom a little too tightly by the arm.

"I want you to know, before this guy says anything," I tell him. "It's going to be about the matter I keep trying to raise with you."

He merely shrugs and nods almost imperceptibly.

Jas is upon Balkar in a flash with a look that would have felled most men. "Get off my drive!" she yells. "You're not welcome here!"

Balkar ignores her and smiling broadly, he turns towards Tom. "Ah! As you can see, it's my turn, Tom. Doesn't it remind you of the welcome she once gave you at the shop?"

Jas looks ready to rush in and do him some harm.

I step forward. "I'll deal with this Jas, *please.*" I tell her.

"You're just out of hospital!" she hisses.

"Had a nasty turn then, have we, Rakki?" says Balkar.

For a second time I hold back Jas.

"Jas, I *said*, I'll handle it! Just take the kids inside." Without once taking her eyes from Balkar, she backs reluctantly to where the children are standing. I turn to face my former friend.

"Look, Balkar -" I begin.

He cuts me short. "It's Tom I'm here to speak with, if you don't mind? You've had your chance, Rakesh." He takes Tom by the elbow. "I'd like a few minutes of your time, my friend – privately – if that's OK? I'm sure you'll find it a matter of some interest."

Tom makes no attempt to follow him. "I've nothing to hide from Rakesh, here."

"Believe me, friend, it would be far better said in private."

We turn at the noise of another vehicle approaching; it's Tom's taxi.

"I'm leaving with this taxi," says Tom, "so if you've something to say, go ahead."

"Remember the Sunday morning when she chucked you out of the shop?" He motions his head in the direction of Jas. "You'd just given Rakesh your lottery ticket to be checked."

"Really?" says Tom.

Balkar opens his arms to embrace the surroundings. "That ticket was a winner; it bought this pile – everything that the eye can see."

To my amazement, Tom is smiling and firmly shaking his head. Balkar's expression becomes a little less certain.

"What I'm *saying*, Pal, is that you held the winning ticket and asked Rakesh, here to check it for you. He kept the ticket, but that money is rightfully *yours!* I'm willing to help you to prove it. He confessed it to me. If we can come to an arrangement, I'll back you with a legally sworn statement."

Astonishingly, Tom has turned away and he's moving towards the taxi. Balkar follows him, uncomprehendingly. Tom gets in and winds down the window. He's still wearing a smile on his face.

"I'm afraid you've got the wrong 'pal', mister. I've never, ever gambled in my life."

Balkar is open-mouthed and I guess I am too – two gaping brown goldfish – if that's not too much of juxtaposition.

"But it *was* your ticket, man – your lottery ticket, I'm talking about. Rakesh told me so himself."

"I'm an ex-alcoholic, Balkar. One bad habit's enough for any man, don't you think?" says Tom. He's still smiling as the taxi pulls away down the drive.

Epilogue

Eight years later

We're waiting for Tom in the foyer of Birmingham Symphony Hall. According to Sangi, it has some of the best acoustics in the world. The whole place was built like an instrument. The roof can be raised and lowered to achieve the optimum quality of sound for any given musical event. They need to get it right tonight – nothing but the best for Sangi's debut with the Birmingham Symphony Orchestra. She's only in the chorus, or whatever name it is that they give to the humble violinists that sit behind the lead violinist, but that's more than good enough for her mum and me.

Tom arrives. He looks as though he might burst wide open with pride. It's not a competition of course, but I'm fairly sure that I could beat him in the bursting with pride championships. God, what a mess that would make of the foyer!

We nod in the direction of Tony Pickles and his divorced mum as they walk through to their seats. Sangi and he are an item again. Apparently they never stopped being an item. They kept in touch all through their separate educational paths. He's working for a

239

Birmingham electronics company and doing quite well, I believe. Sooner or later, he's going to find the courage to come visiting and tell me all about himself. It must be quite daunting for him really. I'm a fully signed-up member of the Khalsa now, so maybe he thinks I'm going to slice his head from his shoulders? Jas and I sometimes have a quiet laugh about it. In truth, if it's what Sangi wants, they'll go forward with my blessing. *Sangita Pickles* – it doesn't exactly slide silver-like from the tongue, does it? I'm not sure what my grandfather would have made of it. It's a different world.

The five minute bell sounds and Tom gives me a nudge. It's time to be seated and hear my beautiful daughter make music. We find the three seats and Jas sits between us. Tom could be her brother; they have such an easy relationship these days. He could be mine too – I'll never be closer to any man. In the early days, I tried again a few times to raise the issue of the winning ticket, but he determinedly changed the subject. He did accept me buying a plant nursery, however. It's held jointly in his name and that of Amal. They work together there every day.

My little Amal. He's *big* Amal now, a good two inches taller than his father. He'll never be 'normal', poor lad, in the way that other guys of his age are thinking of girls and college and sport, but he's happy enough, fulfilled enough. He has his plants and these days, he can make himself understood well enough for his needs. To our great joy, he also has his own flat in a sheltered living complex. Jas and I are there in the background when it counts, and Tom too. I know that he'll need ongoing support, but there's money enough and when the time comes, Sangi will never let him down.

Jas is my right hand, my anchor, the love of my life. She still enjoys her golf and days out with the girls, but these days, there's much more on her plate. We down-sized to a smart four-bed in Hagley to release enough to found our two charities: *Forward*: the hostel for reforming alcoholics in Dudley that Tom and I run, and *Time Out* – the one closest to Jas's heart: our respite centre for the families of autistic children. Jas spends all of her spare time there helping out, but she's never let on that she's the founder-benefactor.

Ain't life busy! I'm running between the Gurdwara, the supermarket, the plant nursery, *Forward* and *Time Out*. I've lost two stone, I raised two and half grand for the Sandwell Heart Unit this year by completing the Dudley Half-Marathon and I've never been happier. Sometimes I even permit myself the vanity of thinking that maybe I'm not such a bad Sikh after all.

As for Tom – he's still doing the lottery. He's never won a penny-piece since he became a reformed character.

But in a way he has.